SPORES

THE CORE: Book One

CRAIG MARLEY

Disclaimer: This book is a work of fiction. The names, characters, places, and incidents are the product of the author's imagination and are used fictitiously. Any resemblance to actual persons, living or deceased, events, or locales, is entirely coincidental.

ISBN: 9798642780879

Interior design by booknook.biz

WARNING

IF YOU DON'T KNOW
WHAT LIES BELOW
IT MAY BE A PLACE
NO HUMAN SHOULD GO

TABLE OF CONTENTS

PREFACE

When the first arrow nipped his left shoulder, "Sharkeye" Park quickly dropped to the boggy rainforest floor. Curled up under a thick canopy of ferns, he looked back and saw his native carriers in full retreat. They had dropped his supplies and raced back to more friendly territory. Now he was alone.

"Fuck," he mouthed, knowing that everything he needed to continue his trek into the highlands of Papua New Guinea would become the property of the savage headhunters who were trying to kill him.

This was not the first time Sharkeye had been the target of an enemy assault. Three years earlier, during WW I, as a warrant officer in the Third Australian Marines, he had been wounded by German soldiers. The thought of dying on the field of battle never really bothered him – it was wartime – history in the making – and he wanted to be a part of it.

But this enemy was different. They were cannibals – native tribesmen whose ancestors had settled in Papua New Guinea forty thousand years ago. They painted their faces with colorful mud, wore feathered headgear and a pig tusk through their nose, and strapped a *koteka* tube over their peckers. These near-naked warriors defended their territory with honor using bows and arrows, stone clubs, and spears. And if they killed you, they cooked your body over a bed of hot coals – ate your organs and flesh – and placed your skull in their spirit house next to the skulls of previous intruders.

Sharkeye cautiously retrieved his Enfield service revolver and leveled the sights on the nearest target. Raising the barrel a fraction of an inch above the painted face, he fired a single 442 caliber round. The sharp percussion spooked hundreds of bats and birds roosting in the canopy, causing many to empty their bowels over the exposed parts of his body.

"Shit!" he said, loud enough for the natives to hear him. He was prepared to kill as many of his adversaries as possible. But his years in the military and knowledge of the native people and their culture had taught him to use a measure of restraint.

At the sound of his first shot the natives retreated into the thick undergrowth, leaving him to deal with the snakes and crocodiles.

*****

Sharkeye later returned to the rainforest with enough supplies to spend four or five weeks searching for gold along Koranga Creek, a tributary of the Bulolo River. His first big strike was in 1921 at Wau – a gold nugget the size of his fist that he found near the junction of Koranga Creek, Edie Creek, and the Bulolo River.

During the following twelve months, Sharkeye and his partner Jack Nettleton recovered *six thousand ounces of gold* – enough to make both men rich and famous.

His discovery marked the beginning of the greatest gold rush in history – bigger than the California gold rush of 1849 and the Yukon gold rush of 1890.

From 1924 to 1928, a handful of daring miners worked the nearby area recovering close to four hundred kilograms (15,000 troy oz.) of gold from shallow deposits along the tributaries and banks of the Bulolo River.

Most of the gold was recovered using traditional hand tools and by panning along the creeks and rivers. Dredging was introduced in the early 1930s.

Naturally, these operations resulted in many conflicts with the indigenous people. And because the white miners had superior firepower, many natives died as a result of their protests and uprisings.

The thirst for gold has never waned. Today, Papua New Guinea has some of the largest operating gold mines in the world and holds some of the biggest reserves yet to be discovered.

*****

It had remained in a state of anhydrobiosis for billions of years – trapped in an iron sarcophagus without nutrients or water – unable to metabolize, to move, reproduce, or grow. It had survived the intergalactic collision and the subsequent journey through deep space and time. It had remained viable, even after the impact with earth and three hundred million years of paralysis.

But now it was free and able to continue toward its genetic destiny. The rain infiltrated its microscopic pores and it began to rehydrate – atom by atom – cell by cell – until the entire fungal mass sprang back to life.

Imperceptibly, dozens of filamentous mycelium tentacles slowly emerged from its body, undulating in a rhythmic motion, growing longer, searching in every direction for its first meal in billions of years. From the mycelium grew the hyphae, even smaller filaments that produced digestive exoenzymes, converting proteins and organic matter into a nutritious chemical goop to be absorbed by the fungus.

As the fungus grew and matured inside its current host, it asexually reproduced with an explosive flowering – ejecting thousands of pathogenic spores into the environment. And, with the help of the wind, these microscopic spores traveled great distances before invading – and eventually killing – their next host.

*****

For eons, the indigenous tribes of Papua New Guinea held a special ceremony called *sangai.* It was the most important event in the life of a teenage boy living in the remote jungles and highlands. It separated the men from the boys – washed away their fears, surmounted pain, and gave those who completed the transition the right to live in the spirit house with the bigmen. It also bestowed upon them the courage and fortitude to fight to the death – to appease their gods – and eat the flesh of their enemies.

CHAPTER ONE

Tatu took a long, deep breath of fresh highland air and looked up to the heavens. It was a glorious view. To the east was a new moon. To the west reigned the majestic heights of the mountains and the mighty rainforests.

Behind the muscular eighteen-year-old was his village – the dominion of the Smaark tribe. They lived a simple life, growing sweet potatoes and raising pigs and chickens. A dozen hand-made dwellings made exclusively from the jungle palms, bamboo, vines, and grasses provided refuge and security. Grey, hand-packed mud sealed the exterior walls and roof against seasonal monsoons. Except for conjugal visits, the women, children, and teenage boys lived alone.

The most prominent edifice in the village was the *gaigo* – the spirit house. It too was fabricated from jungle vegetation and was strategically placed in the center of the settlement. Two carved wood crocodile heads marked the main entrance to the sixty-foot-long complex. The gaigo was the exclusive residence of the bigmen – men who had completed the sangai. It was a sacred place – off-limits to all except by invitation from the bigmen.

"Tatu!" yelled Anaak running as fast as his twelve-year-old legs could muster. Breathing heavily, he shouted, "Bossman Tom want you. He want you gaigo. Hurry. Bossman Tom want you."

"Okay, no need to shout at me." Tatu took a moment to collect his thoughts. He wondered why Bossman Tom wanted to see him. This was a most unusual request from the chosen one – the acclaimed vanguard of the Smaark tribe. Had he offended the spirits? Was he being accused of a crime? A shot of trepidation shot through his body.

"Hurry! Bossman Tom want you gaigo now."

"Okay, Anaak, okay. I will go," he said, breaking into a run. He stopped just short of the first of several steps leading to the entrance and called out. "Bossman Tom. It is me, Tatu."

After a few seconds, a crackling voice cried out, "Tatu, you may enter."

He climbed six bamboo steps and swung open the door – a woven grass mesh stretched across a rectangular bamboo frame. As he stepped into the gaigo, his eyes immediately fixed on his overlord, the most senior and surely the wisest of all the elders.

He was shorter, but more muscular than most of the other elders. It was difficult to guess his age. Tatu thought he might be seventy years old. His dark brown skin loosely covered his aging bones, wrinkled and scarred from decades of perseverance in a land of never-ending hardship and tribal warfare. Hunched over at the waist, with knobby, bow-legged limbs, he clearly was suffering from *boochagari*. His toes were spread wide apart like a cuscus paw, no doubt from spending his entire life without owning a pair of shoes. A scruffy grey beard circled his wide mouth. He seldom smiled, but when he did, he flashed a dozen coal-black teeth – permanently stained from decades of chewing betelnut. From his furrowed neck hung a gut-strung necklace proudly displaying a large cassowary claw surrounded on both sides by a succession of increasingly larger crocodile teeth. A golden kina shell spiraled out from his nostrils across his cheeks. Dressed in a dried grass skirt and a colorful feathered headpiece, he smelled like smoldering pig hair. Tatu briefly considered that one day he might look and smell just like Bossman Tom. It was a repulsive mental image.

"Follow me. I want to show you something," whispered Bossman Tom. "This is one of the secrets I promised when you agreed to complete your sangai and become one of us. The spirits have given me the power to show you this secret, but you must promise not to tell anyone what you are about to see or hear. If you break the promise, bad spirits will take your heart."

A rush of foreboding surged through Tatu's body – his heart began to race. Taking a deep breath, he replied, "I promise not to reveal any secrets."

Tatu followed the elder down the center of the gaigo, through a single bamboo door and into a small parlor. Directly ahead lay a large stone obelisk. Hung along the walls were several rows of human skulls resting on bamboo stakes. Some appeared to have been fractured with a heavy object – a stone hammer or axe. Others were missing several teeth. One had lost his jaw. Tatu took an educated guess as to how many human skulls were on display – thirty or more – trophies from past conflicts. He had no doubts as to whom these skulls once belonged – rapists, murderers, and thieves from neighboring tribes. He looked at Bossman Tom, then back to the skulls – a panorama of primal treasures – a profound piece of Smaark heritage. After several moments, the elder pointed his index finger toward the exit and nodded his head, indicating it was time to leave the secret crypt.

Tatu was vibrating from within. He had heard many stories about tribal warfare and the practice of headhunting and cannibalism. But seeing the skulls of past victims brought these stories to life.

"That was long ago," whispered Bossman Tom, tilting his feather-decorated head toward the secret crypt. "What do you think?"

Shaking the sacred images from his thoughts, Tatu replied.

"When did these men die?"

"Some died long ago – before I came to be. Some in my lifetime. They all died in mortal combat – many for stealing our land, or for raping our women, murder, or killing our pigs."

"When was the last man… eaten?" It was a question he really didn't want answered.

"More than twenty years ago. Now, it is against the law. But it still happens when we must avenge a murder, rape, or the theft of a pig. Today, with the new laws, the punishment for revenge is rarely equal to the deed. Those convicted of killing and eating human flesh are sent to jail for only a few months."

Tatu hesitated to ask the next question, but it somehow slipped passed his lips. "Have you ever eaten human flesh?"

Bossman Tom gave his protégé a piercing stare before responding. "It was our custom for thousands of years. The spirits commanded victorious warriors to eat the flesh of their deceased enemies. They promised it would give them greater strength and power. Now, I am an old man. Soon the spirits will take me. But when I was a young warrior, I did many things according to our customs."

"I don't think I could do that – eat a human – even if I had killed him in battle."

"I don't know if I would do that again. Besides, human flesh tastes bad – like burnt bats and maggots." The elder snickered, then returned to his purpose.

"Come, follow me. I need to talk to you about something very important. Sit here, by the crocodile carvings. It is quiet. No one will hear what we say."

Placing a hand on Tatu's shoulders, he began his recital. "After weeks of beatings, sleepless nights, forced runs, ceremonial dances, snake hunts, and humiliation, you are the only initiate from your group who will enter the gaigo."

Tatu released a sigh of gratitude while his mentor patted him on his shoulder.

"Most of the elders do not understand what is happening to our world. Our people have grown lazy. We sleep more time than we work. The modern world is forcing us to change our ways faster than we can adapt. The miners steal our land and gold. We get little in return. The government makes new rules we must obey or go to jail. The elders do not know how to adapt and have no new ideas. It is time for us to listen to someone who is young, wise and brave. You are that man – the only man in our clan who can see our future."

"But I have not finished sangai. The elders would not allow me to stay with them in the gaigo or listen to my voice. I would not be welcome."

"Your sangai is over. You are the only one capable of joining the elders in the spirit house. I will see to that. But I need your help. There will never be another sangai. Most of our young men want to work in the mines or find a job in the big city. That is why you need to do one more thing – something that will overcome the elders' objections – something they will admire."

"What must I do?"

"Kill a cassowary."

"That is not a difficult task."

"With a bow and arrow."

"A bow and arrow? Why not a shotgun? That's how everyone kills a cassowary today. It is too dangerous to hunt cassowary with a bow and arrow. If they are wounded, they may kill you."

"Anyone can shoot a bird with a shotgun. But a bow and arrow – like we did a hundred years ago – that will get everyone's attention."

*****

The Smaark village bordered on the Jaba river. It was the source of water for drinking, bathing, and transportation to many neighboring tribes. The Jaba allowed the tribes to trade goods and gather for special celebrations. Now, just before the monsoon, the water level in the Jaba was low. It was the end of the dry season. Soon it would rain, and the mosquito infestation would greatly diminish.

Tatu walked toward the riverbank, his eyes scanning a few feet ahead looking for poisonous snakes lurking in the tall grass. He had lost a childhood friend to a puff adder and was naturally on guard. When he reached the water's edge he looked up and down the opposite bank for the tell-tale red eyes of crocodiles. Reasonably sure it was safe, he sat on the grassy shore and extended his muscular legs into the cool water. Using his legs, he pushed apart the floating salvina plants, exposing a pool of clear water. Bending over at the waist, he splashed water over his stomach, chest, shoulders, and face.

"Ahaa," he lightly moaned while examining the painful cuts the bigmen had made on his chest and shoulders. The wounds were healing and would leave lumpy scars that looked like crocodile bites racing across his stomach, around his nipples and chest, over his shoulders and down his back to his waist. He was proud of his ceremonial scars. They provided lifelong evidence of completing the transition from a *bandee* to manhood.

Tatu lay back against the cool grass, closed his eyes and drifted back several weeks to the days when he and the other bandees were suffering through the pain and torment of sangai.

Flesh cutting was the primary means of torture. Using a sharpened piece of bamboo, the bigmen made several rows of crescent-shaped cuts on each initiate. The cutting continued for several days. Fifty to sixty cuts were completed in each session lasting an hour or more. The more cuts the initiate endured, the deeper and longer each flesh-cutting session continued until each initiate had at least five hundred cuts. Then, as the blood flowed freely, each initiate smeared their wounds with grey mud. Infections were covered with *gawk*, a healing oil. Those who cried out or refused to accept the pain were sent home to rejoin their mother and younger siblings.

Day and night, for the duration of sangai, bandees wore a hand-crafted grass apron. Then, after shaving their heads, their hair cuttings were coiled into a round wiglet, topped with bird-of-paradise feathers, and secured to their head with a cord. A large hemp rope encircled their necks like a hangman's noose – a symbol of impurity, allegiance, and obedience.

*****

Sitting on the bank of the Jaba, Tatu considered his cassowary hunting options. He could go downriver, but there would be more hunters in the valleys and probably fewer birds. He could go upriver where there would be more birds and fewer hunters, but the terrain would be steep and there were many more crocodiles. He chose to go upstream and prepared for what he believed might be a long and arduous hunt into the highest, most remote and hostile rainforest. He was an experienced hunter and knew what was required of him to survive for a week or more in the bush.

There was an abundance of fresh water and edible resources in the rainforest. And since he would be traveling upriver, he was unlikely to meet up with adversarial tribesmen. Nevertheless, in the highlands of Papua New Guinea, there were a thousand ways to die.

His primary concern were the silent saboteurs – taipans, puff adders, and blacksnakes. The bite from one of these slithering devils would kill a grown man in less than two hours. And there were the crocodiles, many two meters long or more, who occupied much of the calmer waters of the rivers, lakes, and tributaries.

*****

It was a sunny morning. Tatu stood tall and proud in front of a dugout canoe. He wore a pair of crusty khaki shorts, a ragged T-shirt embossed with the letters PNG and a pair of black sneakers donated by the local Catholic church. A sheathed, eight-inch hunting knife was tied around his waist with a length of hemp rope. He brandished his bow and four arrows in his right hand and a steel machete in the left. Strapped to his back, a small canvas kit contained two sweet potatoes, star fruit, a flint fire-starter, a clump of oily cuscus fur for tinder, a coil of hemp twine, and a small bamboo tube of gawk antiseptic oil.

A large contingent of Smaark villagers, mostly women and children, came down to the river to cheer for their prodigy. Gathered on the grassy shoreline, the villagers chanted and danced to the beat of a pair of slit drums. It was a festive moment and an honorable way to begin the final chapter in his quest for manhood.

Bossman Tom and a few elders sat in silence away from the crowd. Most of them believed the young bandee would likely fail to kill a cassowary or never return. To them, his endeavor was symbolic of their legacy and the troubling future they faced from the overwhelming greed, power, and trajectory of the modern world that was chipping away at the traditions, culture, and spiritual universe the indigenous people had embraced for thousands of years.

After loading his hunting and survival equipment, Tatu climbed into the narrow dugout canoe.

"Anaak. Let's go. We need to paddle upriver to the wild pig trail. That is where we shall say goodbye and I will begin my hunt. You should be back to the village before sunset."

*****

After a three-hour paddle, they arrived at the drop-off point. Tatu secured his equipment and bid farewell to his young friend.

Tatu followed the narrow wild pig trail as it snaked through the jungle canopy until reaching the face of a rocky cliff. He had walked about five klicks. The sun was near the horizon, and it was time to make camp for the night.

Like giant snails, grey clouds crept across the darkening sky, preparing to release a thundering downpour. The monsoon season was looming.

After building a small lean-to and a fire, he ate half a sweet potato and munched a few bites of star fruit. Like every other Smaark, sleeping under the stars was just part of living.

As a day-breaking sunbeam crossed his eyes, he awoke and stretched the stiffness from his arms and legs. Off in the distance, the melodious chirping of a Paradise Kingfisher seeking to attract a mate brightened his spirits. After a worthy *pispis*, he loaded up his gear and began to follow the cliff face up the steep terrain. The higher he climbed, the taller and thicker the trees and plants of the rainforest grew. There was no shortage of building materials or edible plants. But he was looking for a special tree – one that would provide an ideal shooting position – the tallest tree in the rainforest – the *tualang*. It soared skyward as high as eighty meters and provided the best view of the surroundings. The branch of a tualang tree was a perfect place to ambush a cassowary bird.

The flightless cassowary is extremely important to the highland natives. They are often traded for a bride or a pig and signify nobility. Their feathers decorate native bodies and ceremonial headpieces. For highlanders, cassowaries are reputed to possess mystical power, and many believe they are the reincarnation of their ancestors.

Midway through the second day, and eight more klicks into the thick highland rainforest, Tatu came to a river. He took the opportunity to rehydrate and take a short break. The river was clearly subject to seasonal flooding. Dense rainforest grew down to the edge. The shoreline contained piles of dead trees, roots, rocks, and other debris – clear evidence of monsoon flooding. After drinking his fill, he navigated through the dense growth using his machete to clear a path downstream. This was an extremely arduous and time-consuming undertaking and slowed his progress through the rainforest. As he rounded a gentle curve he came upon a widening. The opposite riverbank appeared to consist of gravelly mud. The water was calm and looked to be shallow.

Driven by perseverance, he decided to cross the river where the rainforest was thicker and more likely to be home to big cassowary birds. He cautiously placed one foot in front of the other, testing his footing for quicksand or sticky clay that could pull him under. Fortunately, the bottom was firm, a mixture of rocks and mud, making it easy for him to cross. As he stepped from the water on the opposite bank, he saw a footprint.

"Waahoo," he whispered through puckered lips. "Cassowary prints! And there's another. This might be a good place to hunt."

Continuing downriver along the shoreline, he found several more cassowary prints. Regrettably, he also came upon the footprints of a large crocodile heading away from the stream.

"There's a crocodile nest in the rainforest," he lamented while examining her footprints and the furrow from her tail. He recalled what his father had told him about estimating the size of a crocodile. *"Double the distance from the tip of her tail to the tip of her rear claws."*

"Two meters or more. She's a man-eater. Thanks for the lesson, father."

After walking another hundred meters, counting cassowary prints along the way, he sighted a grove of tualang trees. A rush of adrenaline raced up his arms.

"This is it. This is where I'll take my cassowary," he said with a resolute grin.

Set back from the river was the perfect tree. He dropped his backpack, machete, bow and arrows, and removed his shoes. He then wrapped his arms around the trunk, squeezed his toes firmly into the bark, and slowly shimmied his way up to the first branch overlooking the shoreline.

"Perfect," he muttered as he studied the river and surroundings.

Tatu jumped to the ground and began to make a hunting blind. He gathered some palm fronds, cut them to a suitable size with his machete, and tied them side by side in the curved shape of a battle shield. It didn't take long for him to haul the makeshift blind up the tualang tree and secure it to his shooting position with lengths of hemp rope.

"Don't forget the plums – ripe cassowary plums." He muttered his thoughts. "They must be growing nearby, or the birds wouldn't be here."

He jumped from the tree, secured his machete, and bush-whacked his frame through the thick vegetation. A few minutes later, he found several ripe plums that had fallen to the ground.

After placing a line of plums along the shoreline, he collected his equipment –climbed up to his lair – settled his frame into a tactical shooting position – and waited.

*****

A new moon hung low on the horizon. The night creatures – crocodiles, giant tarantulas, poisonous snakes, centipedes, and thousands of species of insects, came out of their hideaways in search of their evening meal.

Hours passed without any signs of his target and he struggled to remain alert. The branch he was seated upon had squeezed the blood from his left buttock and leg. He shifted his weight to relieve the numbing discomfort, then caught himself just as he was about to lose his balance and fall to the ground. Angered by his imprudence, he steadied himself in a more secure position and listened for audible signs of his target – a koo-koo chirp or a caw-caw mating call.

The new moon had climbed to its apex. Although his arms and legs continued to be painfully numb he remained acutely alert, pinching his earlobe whenever he needed a painful reminder of his mission. With the monsoon came the wind and rain. The rustling of the rainforest made it increasingly difficult to hear his prey. He took a deep breath and thought about what Bossman Tom had said. *"Anyone can shoot a bird with a shotgun. But a bow and arrow – like we did a hundred years ago – that will get everyone's attention."*

It was well past midnight when she magically emerged from the rainforest – camouflaged by her black, grey, and white feathers. She was a majestic creature, a meter tall at the shoulders. Long, red wattles hung from her throat – bobbing from side to side with each of her tentative steps. Admirably sprouting from the top of her head grew a large boney casque shaped like the blade of an axe.

Her unpredictable movements and intermittent strut made her a difficult moving target. He knew he had to make the kill with his first arrow. If he missed, she would disappear into the rainforest long before he could get a second chance to fulfill his obsession. He concentrated all his energy on his target while silently placing an arrow across his bow. He took a long, slow, deliberate breath through his nose and held it in his lungs – waiting for the bird to move closer to the plums.

Looking left and right, the cassowary cautiously took another step – then nervously froze while turning her head into the wind. After a few judicious steps she reached one of the cassowary plums – picked it up in her large beak – tilted back her head and swallowed it whole.

With a rapidly beating heart, Tatu focused all his thoughts and senses on his target. She was the largest cassowary he had ever seen – maybe fifty kilos. Moving less cautiously now, she moved on to the next cassowary plum – ten meters from the tip of the arrow. Stealthily, yet calmly, he raised his bow above the blind and leveled the arrow at the heart of the beast. He could feel the tension in the air – taste the bitter-sweet thrill of conquest.

The arrow erupted from the bow at fifty meters per second, striking the cassowary in the right flank. It forcefully passed through the feathers, skin, and rib cage, perforating the creature's heart. The giant bird leaped two meters into the air – instinctively launched a few aimless kicks… and dropped dead.

"*Ow-a, ow-a,*" shouted Tatu. A wide grin of conquest spread across his face.

A loud crack of lightning streaked across the sky and the deluge erupted. Perhaps it was an omen from the spirits?

This wasn't Tatu first hunt. He had learned his hunting skills from his father when he was old enough to pull a bowstring. One thing his father had taught him: *"Never leave your kill on the ground or it will be dinner for a dragon."*

He jumped to the riverbank, pulled his knife from his sheath and cautiously approached the cassowary. Her body lay on the sand with the tip of his arrow pointing to the clouds. A circular pool of blood spread across the riverbank, weaving its way around the rocks, growing wider as it flowed toward the river.

"Her claws are bigger than those worn by Bossman Tom," Tatu chuckled with a gush of pride. He poked the body with the tip of his knife, a precautionary procedure confirming the creature was dead.

Grabbing the bird by the head, he dragged the carcass into the water and eviscerated the entrails into the current. He then separated the head from the body, washed it free of blood and put it aside as a trophy.

As he worked, the storm intensified. A series of lightning strikes screamed across the rainforest portending the flooding of the river. Tatu realized he did not have the skills or strength to ford the rapidly rising river. It would be foolhardy, especially if he attempted to do so while burdened with his backpack and weapons. He removed both claws as evidence of his kill and except for one cassowary thigh for his own consumption, he left the carcass for the crocodiles.

*****

By mid-morning, he managed to put four klicks under his weathered sneakers. The rain had ceased, momentarily at least, and he was able to get his bearings. Climbing to a higher ridge, he could make out the conical outline of Mount Hagen to the southeast. With an elevation of six thousand meters, this extinct volcano was the most distinctive landmark in the western highlands. He could also see the valleys and ridgelines that marked the general vicinity of the Smaark village. From his viewpoint, he estimated a two- to three-day trek through the rainforest – *assuming he could cross the raging river.*

The monsoon rains continued to flood his route, slowing his progress. Where possible, he followed the riverbank. However, there were many places where a formation of large rocks or jungle growth blocked his path – the shore had been washed away, or the rain-soaked terrain was too dangerous to traverse. As a result, it was necessary for him to chop his way through thick wilderness with his machete.

Exhausted and hungry, shortly before sunset he found a suitable campsite under a large conifer. He fabricated a shelter, roasted and consumed a portion of sweet potato and spent another night hunkered under the proverbial monsoon sky.

By midafternoon of the following day, he arrived at a what he believed to be a suitable crossing point. Spanning the river was a large, moss-covered tree trunk. It appeared sufficiently sturdy and had probably been there for many years. He climbed to the top of the log and tested its stability.

"*Gnee*, the moss is slippery – like the belly of a fish," he muttered. He took another step and looked down at the boiling rapids below. If he fell, he would likely drown. Using his machete as a walking stick, he placed one foot in front of the other… then another, and another. "Almost there," he mumbled.

Like a long rumbling thunderbolt exploding from the heavens, he heard it coming seconds before it arrived. Knowing this part of the world endured some of the most powerful earthquakes, he dropped to his knees and grabbed a branch sticking out from the ancient trunk. As the earth shook violently in every direction, thousands of bats and birds leaped from their roosts, sounding the alarm with tweets, chips, squeals, and squawks. The improvised bridge shook fiendishly for a few seconds, then collapsed into the raging torrent with Tatu straddling the moss-covered trunk.

Magically, he survived the fall, but his struggle for survival was only beginning. He was immediately swept downriver in a swirling torrent of brown water. He was a good swimmer and had experienced small rapids in his youth. But these rapids were monstrous, unlike anything he had encountered before. Repeatedly sucked underwater, dizzy and disoriented, he almost drowned in the turbulent undercurrents. There was no way to escape. His only hope was to ride it out until reaching calmer waters.

The river was relentless. Each time he was sucked underwater, he tumbled over and over while the force of the water squeezed the air from his lungs until his body begged to breathe. Not surprisingly, during the earthquake and subsequent mayhem, his machete, bow, and arrows had been snatched from his grip. But now that his arms were free, he was able to keep his head above the water and swim faster.

To his good fortune, he eventually bobbed into an area of the river where the turbulence had subsided, and he was able to grasp a twisted root protruding from the high embankment. However, the embankment was too high and slippery to ascend. After catching his breath, he released his grip and tried to stay as close to the riverbank as possible.

The river took several turns before widening into a calmer basin. Rounding a long curve in the river, he observed a gently sloping embankment. A scintilla of hope rushed to the front of his perceptions. His hopes for survival were suddenly crushed the moment he saw a huge crocodile leap from the muddy bank into the river. There was no doubt the monster had seen him and was now on the hunt for his next meal.

Tatu began to kick and stroke with every muscle in his body. He knew he could not outswim the crocodile. The powerful tail and hydrodynamic body gave the slippery beast a significant speed advantage. His eyes ballooned when the river abruptly narrowed, the current rapidly increased, and the boiling rapids intensified. Now both he and the crocodile were trapped in the rampage… *and were about to go over a waterfall.*

*****

It seemed like an eternity before the conscious world returned. Lying on his side, his face half buried in the mud along the rocky shoreline, he sluggishly regained consciousness and wiped the crud from his eyes. He was breathing normally – his heart was beating steadily – and he had somehow managed to cross the river. Shaking the vexing spirits from his brain, he took a moment to examine his body for injuries while spitting out a slimy glob of mud, pebbles, and river water. Other than some abrasions and a piercing headache, he was in pretty good condition, but not quite ready to continue his journey. Exhausted, he fell back to the mud, closed his eyes, and thanked the spirits for saving his life.

Tatu awoke with the rumble and vibrations from another earthquake. It was an aftershock – a reminder that the bigger one had knocked him off the log. To the west, the setting sun was creeping down the left flank of Mount Hagen. The horizon was ablaze in a slurry of reds, yellows, and oranges, and the rain had ceased.

Gathering his strength, he stood up and examined his surroundings. Instinctively, he jumped back at the sight of the crocodile stretched out on the muddy bank a few meters from his feet. The rigid body of the giant amphibian was conspicuously distorted, coiled around a large rock. His head was cocked sideways as though he'd been hung by his neck with a rope. A swarm of flying insects whirled around the carcass.

Taking a few unsteady paces toward the crocodile, he found a suitable rock on which to sit. His knife was still strapped to his waist. Inside his backpack, he found the claws, head and thigh of his cassowary and the remains of a sweet potato. He raised his head and refocused on the crocodile carcass. A scheme rattled in his head.

"Crocodile teeth," he bellowed.

Energized by his good fortune, he hurried to the crocodile carcass where he proceeded to remove his teeth – both upper and lower – with his knife. Finally, without pity or remorse, he cut off both of the beast's front legs – dinner for the next two nights or souvenirs for Bossman Tom.

He abandoned the toothless monster and spent the remainder of the sunlight fabricating a shelter. After finding some wood dry enough to burn, he sat down and considered his options. Later, after the sun dropped below the horizon, he cooked the cassowary thigh and a wedge of sweet potato.

The following morning, feeling refreshed and glad to be alive, he looked out over the landscape while he considered the best route home.

Suddenly, as he scanned the horizon, a burst of light hit him in the eyes. It came from a green rock lodged in the mud. He picked up the fist-size rock and examined the source of the glitter.

"Gold. It's gold. The spirits have been most generous," he shouted, jumping and twirling like a crazed cuscus.

He held the hefty, gold-laced rock in his hand while contemplating what riches it may bring. He then cleaned the specimen of mud, placed it in his backpack and set an imaginary course to the Smaark village.

*****

Late in the afternoon, after trekking through the rainforest for two days and nights, Tatu reached the wild pig trail. He still had a painful lump on the back of his head, but his headache was gone. The rain had ceased, and the sun was dutifully warming the earth. Eager to reach his home, he picked up the pace and arrived at the Jaba river shortly before sunset.

"Anaak! Anaak! It's you. You have come to get me. I am surprised."

"Welcome home. Everyone said you were probably dead. But I know different," replied Anaak.

"How long have you been waiting?"

"Since yesterday. You have been gone seven days. I knew you would come home. Get in the canoe. I will take you home. But you must tell me what happened."

CHAPTER TWO

Dawson Elliott grabbed his bag from the overhead bin of the PNG Airlines wide-body jetliner and waited impatiently for the stewardess to open the cabin door. The six-hour flight from his home in Bali to the Jackson International Airport in Port Moresby was three hours late. And even though he had a first-class seat, it felt more like a trip to purgatory.

The corpulent gentleman sitting in the window seat next to him had little regard for his personal hygiene, or the revolting effect he had on nearby passengers. If there had been another seat available, Dawson would have taken it. But the flight was full, and he had no choice but to endure endless rants about how the Papuan government was as corrupt as the miners' union. The newspapers said so, and that constituted prima-facie evidence of their criminality. The odoriferous slob finally ran out of conjecture, fell asleep, and snored his way through the final hour of the flight.

It was seven o'clock in the evening. The international terminal was noticeably quiet. A faint scent of orchids and eucalyptus wafted through the terminal. Dressed in black uniforms and military boots, a conspicuous pair of armed airport police patrolled the concourse accompanied by a no-nonsense black and brown German Shepherd.

After clearing customs and immigration, Dawson took the airport tram to the Hyatt Airport Hotel, one of three places in the world where one might find him.

"Good evening, Mr. Elliott. How was your flight?" asked Bebe, the desk clerk.

"Hi, Bebe. Glad to see you," he said with a smile. "The trip was stinky and boring." He pinched his nose with his right thumb and index finger. "How's your family? Are you a grandpa yet?"

"Yes, our daughter had a baby girl last week. Mother and baby are fine."

"Congratulations. You must be very proud."

"Yes, thank you. Here is the key to your suite. I had room service put an extra ice tray in your cooler and there is a bottle of your favorite scotch in the closet."

"Excellent," replied Dawson, handing him a five-hundred-kina banknote.

"Thank *you*, Mr. Elliott. Please let me know if you need anything."

Dawson took the elevator to the tenth floor and quickly found his regular suite at the end of the hallway. After a glance to the rear, he inserted the digital key card and entered his room. The shades were open, per his request, exposing the picturesque view of the harbor. Mary, his dependable room attendant, had left a small box of Dutch chocolates on his bed and a fresh bouquet of colorful azaleas on the coffee table.

"Jesus Christ, I smell like that fat bastard sitting next to me," he groaned. "I need a shower and a drink."

After shaving his face and head with his electric trimmer, he showered, put on a baby blue, short-sleeve shirt, khaki shorts, and white canvas deck shoes. At 53, six-foot-two and two hundred pounds, Dawson still earned a few smiles from the ladies. Compared to the natives of Papua New Guinea, he was a giant. Placing an LA Dodgers baseball cap on his sheared head, he headed for the Vue Restaurant for a drink and a steak.

"Howdy, Henry," Dawson exclaimed as he settled himself into a seat at the bar. "Break any hearts while I was gone?"

"No sir, Mr. Elliott," Henry chuckled. "How was your vacation? Score any sheilas?"

"Come on, man. What do you think?" he replied with a wink. "It's the national pastime in Bali. The fact is, I did some deep-sea fishing, scuba diving, and spent the rest of my vacation admiring the bikinis on Kuta Beach and reading a good murder mystery. All I can say is I didn't get much reading done."

"What can I get you?"

"Lagavulin, double if you please, mate. And a Perrier over ice. My throat is as dry as the Canberra desert."

Henry poured his friend a generous double and placed it on a bar napkin together with a small bowl of mixed crackers and nuts. He then filled a tall glass with ice and Perrier and set it in front of Dawson.

Dawson gulped half the Perrier, then took his drink in his hand and turned to focus his tired eyes on the harbor. A slight breeze blew across the bay sending rows of pleasure craft on a lazy dance. Mesmerized by the slow-motion pitch and roll, he placed the edge of his glass to his lower lip, tilted his head, and let a stream of malty scotch trickle down his throat. It was a ritual he had practiced for many years.

His reason for being in Port Moresby rushed to the front of his thoughts. As the Managing Director for Keystone Resources, the third largest gold mining company in the world, he was responsible for producing four thousand ounces of refined gold per day, plus the overall performance and safety of two thousand employees. It was a daunting challenge, but one he found very rewarding, both financially and personally.

The only son of an ambitious Redondo Beach trial attorney, Dawson grew up on the beaches of Southern California. His mother taught English to Latino immigrants. He was much more ambitious and adventuresome than his peers – a characteristic he exploited professionally and socially.

With a PhD in mining engineering from Caltech, and over thirty years of experience, he was considered one of the key players in the international gold mining community. And while he enjoyed and excelled in his work, his foremost passion was prospecting for the next mother lode and the thrill of discovery. Wistful dreams of finding another profitable gold deposit somewhere in the unexplored wilderness of Papua New Guinea haunted his restless nights.

He was surprised to hear his cell phone chime, but he recognized the caller.

"Alby Knight. How are you, man? How's the assaying business? Talk to me."

"G'day, mate. Did I catch you in a compromising condition, or are you just having a smoothie?"

"Fuck, mate. You caught me. I just arrived from Bali. I'm sitting at the Vue bar enjoying the view. What's up?"

"I think you're gonna wanna hear this, so listen carefully. Here's the short version of a long story. Last week, this young Egan, Smaark I believe, came into my office here in Wabag with a very interesting rock – probably Cretaceous epithermal. I need to do more tests to determine a more precise geological date and source. It looked a little like the ore body at Keystone. Anyway, this rock, about the size of your fist, was laced with over an ounce of gold – not flakes – a solid vein. The Smaark kid said he found it while on sangai – his boyhood to manhood coming-out ritual. You know more about this cultural shit than me. I asked him where he found it and he said he found it by accident along the bank of a river near a large waterfall. He said he was being chased by a big croc when he fell over the waterfall during a monsoon storm a few weeks ago. He believes the spirits saved his life and the gold-laced stone was his reward for becoming a man."

"Smaark, eh? That's one of the most remote and highest tribal villages in the highlands – about eight thousand feet elevation. How in the hell did he get to Wabag? All the roads are muddy as hell."

"He said he walked three days to the highway, then hitched a lift to Wabag from a trucker."

"Do you have the rock?"

"Why the fuck do you think I called you. Of course, I have the rock. Paid him five hundred kina for it. It's in my safe. I was going to melt it down for the gold but then I thought it might be worth a lot more to someone like you. You're always looking for new deposits – right?"

"Listen, I just got back from vacation. I'm heading up to the mine tomorrow on the company chopper. Can I stop by your place and look at this rock?"

"Okay, that's why I called. You have first option. I know a lot of other folks who might be interested, so… well… you know. See you tomorrow. What time?"

"Noon. I'll buy you lunch."

"Hey, it'll cost you more than lunch if you want this stone."

"Yeah, yeah. I know how this works, Alby. I wasn't born an idiot. It took a few years. But I do appreciate your call and I'll see you tomorrow. Oh, does our Smaark have a name?"

"He goes by Tatu. It means big pig. You know the natives revere their squealing porkers. They swap them for wives, bar-b-que them for celebrations, and use them like money to pay off debts. Pigs are like kina shells – a means of barter and exchange."

"Thanks for the cultural sermon. See ya tomorrow."

Dawson took a sip of his scotch and let the thought of discovering a major gold deposit in the highlands of Papua New Guinea ignite a fire in his never-ending quest for the next – the biggest – the most profitable gold mine on the planet. He knew the odds were not in his favor. It just didn't happen that way. At least that was what his decades of experience had taught him. He reached up and wiped the sweat from his brow. The room temperature was tolerable, but the humidity was sticky, and he suddenly felt a little woozy. He took another swig of his ice water and washed it down with his scotch. It must have been the euphoria of a new gold strike rushing through his head. The old-timers called it "gold fever."

Lost in his thoughts, he was just about ready to order another drink when a familiar voice called out. "Well, well, well, look who's here. Dawson Elliott – the man with the golden touch. How about buying a lady a drink?"

Dawson recognized the southern accent. He had heard it many times.

"Cece Whitman. What the hell are you doing in Port Moresby? I thought you were digging for rare dirt somewhere in Vietnam. Please sit with me. Tell me what you're up to. Barkeep, this lady needs a drink. What's your poison?"

"Jack and Coke," she replied, moving a black leather bar stool closer to Dawson. "You look like you're having fun. I mean you look great. Still trying to compete with the young buckaroos, eh? And look at those shoulders. Wow, I am impressed. You must be working out. And you've shaved your head."

Cece Whitman was a rebel debutante, quick-witted and a bit sassy. Born and raised in Atlanta, her brains, stunning beauty, and engaging manner helped her quickly move up the social and academic ladders. She was surely one of the smartest young ladies at Georgia Tech – and proved it by earning a doctorate degree in earth sciences. At five feet, nine inches tall, with silky auburn hair, baby-blue eyes, and a centerfold figure, she had her pick of the litter.

"I shaved it off," he said, lifting his baseball cap and rubbing his open palm over the top of his scalp. "The bugs thought it was a playground, so I did what most ex-pats do, I shaved it off – clean as a baby's bottom." Dawson returned her smile. "You look terrific, Cece. As beautiful and alluring as ever. It's great to see you again. I missed you, too. You know that, don't you?"

Not wishing to go down the reconciliation road, she mollified her response. "It's always nice to see a friend."

"Last time I saw you was at the Earth Sciences Symposium in Brussels last year. You gave a paper on rare earth deposits in China and Chile. I understand they're hoarding all the good stuff." Dawson tried to keep the conversation professionally light – but he could feel his heartrate soar.

"Yeah. Sorry we didn't have time to chat. I was flat-out on overdrive. You're right about the Chinese and Chileans. They produce about ninety percent of the strategic elements – neodymium for super magnets – lithium for batteries – yttrium for high-power lasers – and samarium for nuclear reactor control rods. They know how to manipulate the market price too. Bastards. They own it all and control the market. It's a serious problem for the free world."

"What's with Vietnam?" He momentarily took control of his rapidly beating heart, but the lubricious curl of her red lips wouldn't let up on the throttle.

"They're much more willing to work with us. They want our exploration and processing technology but don't particularly want to sell their souls to a greedy partner. They don't have a clue as to what they have in the ground or how to recover and process it into market-grade product."

"Makes sense. So, what brings you to Port Moresby?" The words came out of his mouth while his mind slipped back to another place and time. For a second, he thought Cece might sense he was not paying attention, so he studied her eyes while pretending to be more interested in her work than her charms.

"The Interior Minister invited me to give a presentation to his staff. I spent two days with them. They have a small exploration group but lack the expertise. My work is done but I'm staying here at the Hyatt for a few days of sightseeing. They may call me back. In fact, I hope they do, but I'm not holding my breath. Enough about me, what about you?"

"Same as always. Managing the mine takes most of my time. We're producing four thousand ounces of gold a day – every day – that's about eight million dollars a day. Frankly, we're seeing a decline in ore quality. Three years ago, we averaged twelve grams per metric ton. Now, we're lucky to get six. We just took delivery of four new loaders at a million dollars each. These monsters can carry a two-hundred-ton load from the bottom of the pit to the processor all day long. We've got to keep the stockholders happy."

"I hope you're not spending your time watching truckloads of ore spinning up and down the pit," she jested with a snicker. "I didn't mean to be flippant. I'm sure you're enjoying the challenge. I mean, I hope you enjoy your work. Aw, fuck it. You know damn well what I mean."

"Yeah. I think I do."

There was an uneasy pause in the conversation. With a generous swallow, Cece finished her drink and crafted a dutiful smile. "Bartender, I'll have another Jack and Coke, please."

Cece wasn't sure about her feelings for Dawson. A few years ago, they had met for the first time at a conference and were instantly attracted to each other. They both were recovering from a bad marriage and somehow found themselves sharing a two-night tryst at the Hyatt Regency in Newport Beach. They kissed goodbye at the hotel and promised to keep in touch. She returned to her work in the Mojave Desert and he dashed off to his gold mine in Papua New Guinea. Neither of them made any promises, but she had hoped there might be something special between them, and that he might call or drop her a note. Sadly, that never happened, and she was mad at herself for being so presumptuous.

"Why didn't you call or write?" she suddenly barked.

Surprised by her bluntness, Dawson jerked back, trying to think of what to say. The words didn't come easy. She didn't say another word – just waited for his reply. He finished his drink in a long gulp and lifted his glass for a refill.

"I… I was scared. It didn't seem possible to have a long-distance relationship. I didn't… I couldn't… I didn't want either of us to suffer heartache again. I believed you would find someone you could love and who would care for you and be by your side every day. I didn't think I was the right man for the job. All I can say is I'm sorry." Dawson choked on his words.

After hearing his confession, she wiped the moisture from her eyes, placed her hand on his and squeezed it tenderly. "I was scared too," she said with trembling lips. They both hung on to the moment and slowly realized the spark might still be alive.

"You should see the site. We've dug the deepest open-pit mine in the world – over fifteen hundred meters deep and six klicks wide. We've been digging this monstrosity for over twenty years. However, I think we'll be pulling the plug in a year or two. We desperately need to find another high-yield ore body – hopefully nearby. If not, I'll be out of a job. Maybe I could go to work for you?"

"Dawson, as much as I love ya, and you know that I always will, that would never happen. We had some wonderful moments together and I cherish the memories. But you and I… well… I don't think we could work together. We'd be bickering from the start. You'd storm out the door and I'd cry myself to sleep. Nope. Never happen."

Dawson pursed his lips, wrinkled his brow and nodded his head. "You're right, Cece. But I do have a proposal that is definitely more entertaining than a smelly bus tour."

"Okay, I'm game."

"I've got to take the company chopper to Wabag in the morning to inspect a stone. Some young indigenous tribesman found a gold-laced nugget somewhere out in the highland rainforest. He sold it to my assayer friend Alby Knight. Alby offered me an opportunity to examine it and said he would sell it to me if I wanted more tests. After that, we can head up to the mine. I'll show you around, introduce you to some incredible people and buy you lunch. I think you'll learn a lot about how we open-pit gold miners work in PNG… and it won't cost you a single kina."

"Sounds great. Listen, I'd love to sit and chat, but I'm exhausted and need to get some shut-eye. What time are you leaving?"

"I'll be in the hotel restaurant at eight. We'll take the hotel shuttle to the business airport. Depart at nine – arrive Wabag at eleven. If we visit the mine, I'll have you back to the hotel by seven. But just in case we get stuck overnight… you know… pack accordingly."

*****

Cece was serving herself a bowl of fresh fruit when Dawson appeared in the hotel restaurant.

"Hey, lady. I'm so glad to see you. May I assume you are joining me?"

"I wouldn't miss it. How are we doing on time?"

"No worries. The chopper will wait for us."

After breakfast, they took the shuttle to the business airport.

"There's our bird. Red, white, and blue. Sikorski twin turbo. She's the best air taxi you can fly in PNG. Two hundred miles an hour, six passenger comfort, big viewing windows. I think you'll be impressed. Teddy, my chief pilot, is the best tree-top bush pilot in the business and my best friend."

Born and raised in Baton Rouge, Teddy Mitchell grew up in a large family. With six younger brothers and sisters, his parents expected him to set respectable examples of behavior and exhibit a strong moral compass. His father was a veterinarian, which allowed his mother to remain a full-time matriarch, caregiver, and cheerleader for the Mitchell clan. After earning a degree in aeronautical engineering, he joined the Coast Guard. They taught him how to fly, to hunt hurricanes, and rescue survivors from sinking vessels. After his discharge, he took any job that offered good pay and an adrenaline-pumping lifestyle. Chasing rainbows in the rainforests of Papua New

Guinea filled the bill. He was married once, but she shortly found it impossible to compete for his affection against the call of the wild. One day she packed her bags and left him for a dentist.

The flight to Wabag was uneventful. The weather was clear with a few cumulus clouds. After departing Jackson airport, the terrain segued from skyscrapers to industrial parks, to high-rise apartments – all surrounded by a dismal ring of shantytown slums. Beyond, lay the rainforest, the highlands, and hundreds of villages of indigenous tribes – many of which still believed in – and occasionally practiced – cannibalism.

*****

Alby set up his assaying business in a modern industrial park a short drive to the airport. The back of the property was surrounded by a chain-link fence, which, unfortunately, didn't stop the midnight thieves from stealing whatever junk or rubbish had been left outside.

Dawson paid the cabbie with a twenty-kina bill and helped Cece exit the cab.

"Alby, are you back there?" Dawson shouted after entering the assayer's office. "It's me, Dawson. I have a friend with me. We're here to see the rock."

"Hey, Dawson, I'm in the back. I'll be there in a sec. Gimme a minute to get the rock."

Dawson and Cece could hear Alby cussing at his safe.

"He must have forgotten the numbers or mis-dialed them," said Dawson.

"Got it," shouted Alby.

In rubber boots, Alby's footsteps thumped indignantly across the concrete floor.

"Dawson, glad you could come." Casting his eyes up and down Cece he flirtatiously suggested, "Dawson, you rascal. You didn't tell me you were bringing a movie star."

"Cece and I go back a few years. She's a rare-earth specialist."

"I'm honored to meet your acquaintance, your highness," Alby jested with a wide grin and a fleeting bow.

Cece took the chivalrous greeting in stride. She lowered her chin ever so slowly and replied. "Thank you, brave knight. We've come to see your... rock." Giggling, she choked on her words.

Holding out his left fist, he slowly exposed the rock. "Fine, lady, here is the rock. I hope it is what you are seeking."

"Alby, we all know you are the greatest tease. Let me see that rock."

Alby did his best to carry on the Romeo and Juliet charade, but lost it to a belly laugh as he handed Dawson the rock.

"Holy cow. That's one heavy rock. Have you completed any tests?"

"Yup. Got all the data in this file. The first thing I did was an XRF, you know, x-ray fluorescence. It's fast, accurate, and non-destructive. It's almost pure gold, twenty-three carats. The balance is silver. I also ran surface analysis for contamination and corrosives – then infrared spectroscopy to identify organics, carbonates, sulfates, nitrates, ad nauseam. After that, I did a TMA, thermal expansion vis-à-vis temperature and measured the melting point. Finally, I completed a metallographic analysis to examine the grain size, phase distribution of the host material, density, and voids. It's all documented in this file." Alby handed Dawson a thumb-drive. "The host rock is definitely cretaceous – well over a hundred million years old."

"What about this green colored material? I've never seen anything like it," asked Dawson.

"I have. However, I'm stumped as to how it got here. Believe it or not, it's nephrite –pure jade. Jade is the lucky stone. It helps its owner realize their full potential, brings wealth and love and helps lovers resolve any emotional issues."

Dawson looked at Alby, then turned to Cece. "It's our lucky stone – yours and mine. I'm so glad you joined me today."

"Me too," she whispered.

"Okay, how much for the stone?"

"It's yours. Keep it. I appreciate your business and friendship for all these years."

"Thanks, Alby. But please send an invoice for your time and expenses. I owe you. How can I get in touch with the young man who found it?"

"Have your secretary, Jojo, call the Enga provincial government office. They will be able to help you."

"Well, Cece, I guess that's all we need from Alby right now. How about joining us for lunch?"

"Thanks, but no can do. I've got more work to do. Besides, you two should be alone. Nice to meet you, Cece." Pausing for a moment, he declared, "You know, I love your name, Cece. Reminds me of a kitty cat I had as a kid. Her name was Cece. Did you ever have a cat?"

"No. I'm not fond of pets. I do want to ask you something. Do you have any experience with rare-earth elements?"

Alby touched his index finger to his temple and faked a moment of mentation. "No, I don't recall having experienced any rare-earth elements. I did have an experience with a rare-earth lady one night. Does that count?"

Cece winced, then quickly understood Alby's jocularity and erupted in laughter. "You are one sick rascal, but it was a pleasure meeting you."

Dawson led the way to a nearby restaurant while retrieving his smartphone.

"Jojo. It's Dawson. How's everything at the mine?... Good. Listen, I'm in Wabag and need to find the location of the Smaark tribal village. That's Smaark with two a's. Would you please call your contacts at the Enga provincial office and see if they have the GPS co-ordinates? And ask if there is a nearby helicopter landing site. I'll wait for your call. I'd like to fly up there this afternoon if possible."

CHAPTER THREE

"G'day, Teddy. This is my longtime friend, Cece Whitman. Don't let her good looks fool ya. She's one smart lady – doctorate in rare-earth materials. We go back a few years and I promised to show her a good time sightseeing."

"My pleasure, Ms. or Mrs.?"

"Nice to meet you too, Teddy. And I'm single – thank God."

"Change of plans, Teddy. We're not going to the mine. We're going to a remote Enga tribal village in the central highlands – Smaark village. Here's the GPS co-ordinates. There's a helicopter landing site next to the village. It's about thirty miles northwest of the mine at an altitude of about eight thousand feet, next to the Jaba river."

"If everyone is ready, climb aboard and make yourselves cozy."

Cece followed Dawson up four steps to the passenger cabin. A mixture of excitement, intrigue, and danger filled Cece's perceptions. She quickly took a seat on a soft leather seat, buckled her seatbelt and let the anticipation of the moment tease her senses.

"Here's your headset. Put it on and push this button to speak to me," said Dawson. "This bird is a bit noisy – twin turbo engines – a thousand horsepower. You'll hear the pilot instructions and points of interest with these. Keep your seatbelt fastened too. Okay?"

"Sure. I'm good to go."

"Great. Now here in Wabag, the elevation is six thousand feet. The tallest peak in PNG is Mount Wilhelm at about fifteen thousand feet. The Smaark village is at eighty-one hundred feet. Keep those figures in mind as we cruise up and down the valleys and mountains. Most of the time, we'll be flying below the mountains, but don't worry. Teddy is the very best bush pilot. He won't make any dangerous maneuvers. Got it?"

"Yeah, I got it. I hope it's not too bouncy. I don't want to lose my breakfast."

Dawson cupped his headset over his ears and spoke to Teddy. "Let's show Cece some of the wilderness – the Teddy Mitchell version."

Teddy keyed his intercom to announce their departure. "Buckle up and hang on, folks. We're about to lift off."

As the twin turbo engines gained power, the dissonance drowned out natural voice communications. Moments later, Teddy engaged the massive rotors, sending a cyclone of dust, grass, leaves, and twigs racing across the asphalt tarmac.

"Make sure your seatbelt is tight. Teddy likes to give newcomers a few surprises."

With the twin turbos screaming and Cece's heart racing, the chopper lifted off the tarmac and soared upward, where it leveled off at three thousand feet above Wabag.

The view was breathtaking. The terrain was covered in thick groves of vegetation, tall groves of bamboo, two-hundred-foot-high conifers, tree ferns, and giant climbing vines. The peaks of the mountains, many of them exoskeletons of ancient volcanos, soared upward like giant pyramids until they disappeared into the clouds. Below snaked the Lai River winding its way from the snow-capped peaks until it joins the Sepik, the longest river in PNG. The Sepik eventually empties into the Bismarck Sea about sixty miles south of Wewak.

Mesmerized by the phenomenal panorama, Cece lost track of time.

When the helicopter passed over a rocky peak, Teddy abruptly pushed the nose of the aircraft downward into a deep river valley. For a few seconds, Cece thought her stomach might sink to her knees.

"Whoa! What's happening! Are we going down? Oh, God!" she shouted. But no one heard her. She forgot to push the talk button.

Teddy held the dive until they were about five hundred feet above the canopy – then leveled out and sped up the river.

Teddy's voice came over the intercom. "That's the Jaba river below us. It winds its way through these valleys and eventually joins the Sepik.The Smaark village is located on the river. We'll be turning west and should be landing soon."

As the helicopter approached the Smaark village, Teddy dropped toward the village and began to circle the settlement. This was a customary procedure to let the villagers know visitors intended to land. Meanwhile, Dawson continued to keep Cece apprised of the sequence of events as they developed.

"We always announce our intention to land by circling the village. This gives the villagers an opportunity to prepare for our visit and make sure none of their children are playing near the landing zone. We will probably be greeted by some of the village elders. Don't be alarmed if they appear hostile. This is their land and they want to make sure we understand that we are just visitors."

Teddy announce their arrival. "Please make sure your seatbelts are secured. We'll be on the ground shortly."

As the helicopter moved closer to the landing pad, Cece looked out the window and pressed her talk button. "Dawson, there are four men out there – with paint on their faces. They aren't smiling. They don't look happy to see us. Are you sure this is safe? It looks like they have weapons. Do they still kill and eat people? One has a shotgun, two have machetes, and one has a bow and arrows. What are we going to do? I'm not going out there. It's too dangerous." Cece's dizzying rant was a sure giveaway of her trepidation.

"Trust me, Cece. I would never put you in harm's way. This is their traditional greeting. They paint their faces, put on their jewelry, and try to look intimidating. I've done this hundreds of times – paid visits to many remote tribes. I've never been threatened or harmed in any way. Besides, they know I bring gifts – cigarettes, bubble gum, cooking utensils, and toys."

"This is a new experience for me. I'm sorry, but I've got the jitters. Now I know what it's like for a foot soldier waiting for the whistle to charge the enemy trenches."

While the helicopter descended, the foot-tall grass was blown flat in a circular pattern. Immediately after landing, Teddy switched off the engines and waited for the blades to stop spinning before speaking.

"Here we are. Smaark village. Looks like they sent a welcome party."

"Are you sure? They look like warriors to me," Cece stammered.

Dawson attempted to quell her suspicions. "They are warriors, Cece. Think of them as the US Naval Academy color guard carrying an American flag at the Army/Navy football game. We are not their enemy. Just stay back and watch for a minute… please."

Teddy left his seat, opened a small closet and retrieved a plastic tub filled with gifts for the villagers.

"Here you are, boss. You're the diplomat. I'll keep the lights on for you." Teddy kept a forty-five automatic strapped to his side – just in case.

Dawson had met the village elders from dozens of PNG tribes. It was all part of his job – make friends with the natives, treat them with respect, and assure them that your intentions are factual and will benefit them.

Dawson grasped Cece by the arm and escorted her to the exit. "Stay a few feet behind me during the introductions. I'll let you know when it is okay to take photos."

He picked up the box of gifts, exited the helicopter and approached the greeting party. Cece followed as instructed.

Placing the box at the feet of the elders, Dawson introduced himself. "My name is Dawson Elliott. I am the boss man for Keystone Resources. We operate the Keystone gold mine. I believe some of your young men work at our mine. They are very good workers and we want them to be happy. These gifts are for you and your people."

Standing not more than five-foot-five, the Smaark warriors were dressed in resplendent ceremonial colors. Their faces were hand-painted with red and yellow clay. Each man wore a multicolored feather headpiece and a headband made from dried green beetles and cowry shells. Strings of cassowary claws and crocodile teeth encircled their necks – a wild pig tusk or crescent-shaped kina shell curled upward from their nostrils.

While the Smaark greeting party rummaged through the gift box, Cece couldn't help noticing the obvious.

She hurriedly closed the gap between herself and Dawson, then whispered in his ear. "What is that thing sticking out of their... crotch?"

Dawson tried to hold back the giggles, but the scene was just too hilarious to maintain his decorum.

Reeling inside, he choked on his reply. "That's called a koteka. It's a penis gourd." Dawson held up a finger, begging for a moment to regain his composure. "The men... they wear them on special occasions. They know... white women will be shocked."

Tears of laughter streamed down his cheeks which he promptly wiped away with his shirt sleeve. "That's one reason they wear them. You should feel honored."

Trying not to be insensitive, Cece covered her mouth with her hand and shook her head. "Jesus, they're so long, and pointed too. God, I hope their pecker or Willy or Johnson or whatever they call it... you know... isn't the same shape or size as the coat hanger... or whatever you call it. Ouch!"

"It's called koteka, not coat hanger. Koteka singular or plural. Koteka. Say it."

"One Koteka, two koteka, three koteka, four. I got it. It looks like an ice cream cone without the ice cream."

The Smaarks didn't seem to be moved by Cece's reaction. They just looked at the box of goodies with their erect koteka pointing skyward.

Dawson explained further. "Koteka are made from a sun-dried gourd. They grow on a vine like string beans. The natives secure them against their crotch with a cord around their waist and elevate the tip with another cord tied around their neck. The tighter the cord, the higher the tip of the koteka. It's a guy thing."

"I know it's a guy thing, but I can see their scrotum. Their balls are... oh, well... it is what it is. Give me a few minutes. I'll get used to it." Cece chuckled but couldn't help herself from watching the bouncing koteka.

One of the elders took the lead. "My people call me Bossman Tom. This is Ram, one of our elders. He smoke Marlboro. He thank you for the Marlboro."

"I hope he enjoys them," replied Dawson.

"This man is Yanun. He is elder. He smoke Marlboro sometime, but chew betelnut most of the day."

"And this man is Tatu. He is young and very courageous. He is now a man. He does not smoke Marlboro or chew betelnut."

"I wish to speak with Tatu. He sold a green rock with gold to my friend in Wabag. I want to hear his story about the rock. We will pay you and Tatu if he will show us where he found the rock."

"Who is the woman? She is big woman. Is she your wife?"

"Her name is Cece. She is a scientist like me. We are friends. She is not my wife. She has never been to PNG before. But she is a good friend to everyone."

"Why do you wish to see where the rock was found?"

"The Keystone mine is running out of gold. You know because your village received less money for the past few years. We need to find another mine to pay you more money. If Tatu found a rock with gold, there may be more gold nearby. It may become another mine, like Keystone. But we must find it first."

"I speak with elders."

Dawson turned and smiled at Cece while the men openly discussed the opportunity. They spoke with a combination of broken Australian Pidgin and native Smaark. A few of the words and phrases sounded Japanese; they had occupied parts of Papua New Guinea during World War II.

After a few minutes, the men nodded in agreement.

"Tatu will help you. What do you want him to do?"

"We want him to show us where he found the rock. We want to go there in the helicopter. I will pay him for his time. I will pay you and your people for your help."

The elders gathered once again. After another minute or so of pidgin talk, they all nodded in agreement.

"How much will you pay?"

"Five thousand kina for Tatu to show us where the rock was found. Ten thousand kina for your people."

"We have one other request. We must all go in helicopter. We will talk to the spirits. The spirits will help you find the gold."

"That is a very good idea. Please, everyone, follow me."

"Wait. Money first."

"Yes. Of course." Dawson retrieved three, five-thousand-kina notes from his wallet and presented the money to Bossman Tom and Tatu. "We thank you for your help."

The elders laughed, shouted and jumped up and down like a bunch of second graders playing hopscotch.

Tatu simply smiled and boarded the helicopter. The elders soon followed.

"Hey, what's going on?" asked Teddy.

"We're going to find the gold. This young man, Tatu, will show us where he found the rock."

"I want him in the cockpit with me. I've flown over these highland rainforests hundreds of times. Maybe he can give me a quick summary, and I can get us there straightaway."

Tatu entered the cockpit – dazzled by all the dials and instruments. "Thanks for joining me. Have a seat in the co-pilot chair. Tell me the story of your journey."

"I took canoe up the village river to a wild pig trail. It is on the other side of the Jaba river. I walked wild pig trail until I found the cliffs."

"Whoa. Stop. That's way too complicated. Here's a topo map of Enga province. It shows the major landmarks, villages, roads, rivers, and waterfalls." As he spoke, Teddy pointed to the features on the map with his index finger. "Here is the Jaba river and the Smaark village. Here is Mount Hagen. The thin lines surround a mountain. Take your time. See, here is the Smaark village on the Jaba river. And here is the big river. It is called the Lagaip. It's north of your village. When it rains this river is very dangerous and there are several waterfalls. The biggest waterfall is Gemini Falls. It's a fifteen-meter drop from the top. You can see it on the map. You and the crocodile probably went over this waterfall. That is my best guess. If I am correct, you are a very lucky man. You can talk to me as we fly – tell me if we are going to the place you found the gold rock. Here, put on this headset. Press the black button to talk to me. Look at the map as we fly toward the big waterfall."

Tatu fastened his seat belt, put on his headset, and began to study the topo map. Teddy fired up the twin turbojets and engaged the rotor while Cece and Dawson showed each of the elders how to use their headsets. A minute later they were airborne and headed for the rainforest.

Dawson looked at each man and offered a thumbs-up sign. Everyone smiled and copied his gesture. He pressed the comm button. "Tatu, are you okay? Press the number button to speak with me."

"Yes. I am good. This is first time in flying machine. It is loud and fun."

"Teddy will go where you tell him to go."

"Teddy gave me topo map. I'm looking at it now. I think he knows the waterfall."

"Great. I hope you enjoy the flight."

Tatu returned to the map, mumbling aloud as he mentally retraced his journey. "I traveled north most of the time, crossed a river. I killed my cassowary on the other side of the river. When the rain came, I could not go back." He moved his index finger along the Lagaip and continued reciting his recollections of the journey. "I fell into the water during the earthquake here. I went down the river to here. Then the crocodile attacked me here. Yes! Like you said. Gemini Falls. This is where I woke up on the river. This is where I found the rock," he shouted, pointing to Gemini Falls.

"I thought that might be the place. Congratulations. You did a great job navigating. We will be there in about ten minutes."

As they flew deeper toward the river, the vegetation gradually changed from palms, ferns, pines, and broadleaf evergreens to moss-covered hardwoods, conifers, alpine meadows, and tree ferns.

"Ladies and gentlemen. If you look to your right, you will see dark clouds rolling in from the west. We may experience some turbulence, so please make sure your seatbelts are securely fastened. We will be over the target area in about ten minutes."

Teddy descended to within fifty feet of the Lagaip river, then slowly turned east and approached the waterfall.

"Tatu," he shouted. "Do you remember this – just before you and the crocodile went over the waterfall?"

Tatu began to tremble. The sight of the water cascading over the falls rekindled a terrifying image from his memory. "Yes, this is where I almost joined the evil crocodile spirits. But the good spirits saved me."

"I guess the spirits did not like the crocodile. Now we will go down the river. Let me know if you recognize the place where you found the rock."

Teddy continued downriver, slowing his forward speed while Tatu studied the river and surrounding rainforest.

"There it is." Tatu shouted triumphantly. "The bones of the crocodile are still there. This is it. This is where I found the gold."

CHAPTER FOUR

It had been a wild party – a celebration of possibilities. The revelry was more about the cassowary kill and dead crocodile than the highly unlikely prospects of striking a new ore body the size and quality of Keystone. Nevertheless, it was cause for celebration.

A few villagers, women and children, had greeted the returning helicopter with flowers. Tatu, Bossman Tom and his troupe of elders quickly leaped to the ground and addressed their people. The news quickly spread throughout the village and soon there were dozens of Egan villagers surrounding the helicopter, chanting and dancing to the beat of a pair of slit drums. Groups of children joined hands forming a circle, then hopped about like crickets while chanting praise to the spirits.

Cece was jubilant, laughing and loudly chatting amongst the villagers, shaking her head up and down, joining hands with the circle of dancing children, looking and acting like she had just won a mega-million lottery. The atmosphere was intoxicating.

"Dawson," Cece shouted. "I've got to get some pictures. You and Teddy, stand in front of the helicopter. Tatu," she called out. "Please, come now. Take picture with Dawson and Teddy." She held up her smartphone and began to click away. "Bossman Tom, please come," she beckoned, waving her arm. "Bring Ram and Yanun: I will take your picture." Teddy arranged the men in a line near the cockpit and asked them to smile at the camera.

After the photo session, Dawson approached Tatu, placed his arm over his shoulder and shook his hand. "You did a great thing today. You should be very pleased. I know Bossman Tom and your people are proud of you. Maybe one day we will meet again. But we must go now – back to Wabag. Alby. You remember Alby. You sold him the rock. He is my friend. He told me your story. That is why we came to your village to see you. Thank you, Tatu. And may the spirits be kind to you and your people."

The trio continued rejoicing on the flight back to the Wabag airport. Dawson called his favorite Wabag hotel, made reservations, and arranged for the hotel limo to pick up the three weary travelers when they arrived.

"How about a drink? I'm buying," asked Dawson as he registered at the front desk.

"I'm pooped," said Teddy. "I'm going to bed. What time are we going to the mine tomorrow?"

"Yeah. What time do I have to get up?" asked Cece.

"We should leave by ten. Our day won't be as rowdy as today, but I guarantee it will be interesting. Teddy, you did a great job today. Many thanks."

"Yeah, Teddy. Many thanks. That was the most exciting helicopter ride of my life. Thanks for getting us home safely."

Cece tugged at Dawson by the hand and led the way into the hotel. "We need a quiet room with a big bed and a view."

*****

Dawson woke early, leaned over and kissed her on the forehead. "Hey, Cece, it's time to get up. It's time to fly… wheeee." He raised his hand and waved it over her breasts like a jetfighter.

"What time is it?" Cece opened one eye, leaving the other buried under her pillow.

"Almost nine. That was some party, eh?"

She turned her head, exposing her other eye. "It was amazing. The villagers were crazy." She sat up, revealing her naked breasts, then combed her fingers through her hair while shaking her head from side to side. "Did you have a good time?"

"The village party or after we went to bed?"

"The village party was a new experience for me. And last night was great – just like before. Our bodies are like a puzzle. The pieces have to fit to see the big picture."

"We need to get going. My living quarters are quite comfortable, and private. But I'll arrange a separate room if you wish."

"Oh, Dawson, I'm not sure we should… you know… continue trying to solve this puzzle. It's like Rubik's Cube. We keep turning the colors around hoping someday, somehow, they all line up. That doesn't mean I didn't enjoy the party, your company or the sex, but…"

"Shhhh. Come on. Get dressed."

"I need to shower. I'll meet you in the coffee shop in thirty minutes."

"Great. I'll do my best to make you comfortable. In the meantime, I've got to call my office."

Cece quickly showered, put on a fresh face, brushed her hair and dressed. She checked her phone for messages. There was one from the PNG Interior Minister's office. She instantly dialed their number.

"Hello, this is Cece Whitman, I'm returning your call."

"Thank you. The Minister would like to meet with you next week. He wants to discuss a project. I believe you know what he means. Are you available next week?"

"How about next Wednesday, two o'clock."

"That will be fine. I will let the Minister know."

"Great. See you next Wednesday. Goodbye."

Cece was ecstatic. It was the call she had hoped would come.

Meanwhile, after a quick shower and shave, Dawson sat on the bed and called his office. "Hi, Jojo. It's me."

"Good morning, Mr. Elliott. What can I do for you today?"

"I'm in Wabag. Teddy and I will be leaving for the mine in about an hour. I have a female guest. Can you arrange a private room for her?"

"Sure. No problem. I'll have Lucy put some fresh flowers in her room. Anything else?"

"I need authorization from the Enga provincial government to explore a block of rainforest along the Lagaip river – west of the Gemini Falls. We've got to complete an aerial survey, ground penetrating radar and magnetics, the works, then put boots on the ground to clear an area for chopper landings and a core drilling team. I expect the clearing and coring will take a couple of months. I'm texting the GPS co-ordinates to you now. Do you need any other information?"

"No, sir. I'll get right on it. I should have a verbal approval by tomorrow afternoon."

"Thanks, Jojo. This is urgent. I'll be at the office by noon."

Dawson met Cece in the hotel coffee shop. They poured cups of coffee and took a table. She carried the smile of a teenage girl on prom night and Dawson thought she had perhaps decided they still had a chance at a long-term relationship.

Cece picked up a spoon and began to stir the steaming cup. "Listen, something has come up. I had a message from the Interior Minister. They want to discuss a project. I have a meeting scheduled for next Wednesday in Port Moresby."

Momentarily disappointed, Dawson managed to put on a happy face. "Well, congratulations. You obviously made a good impression. Are you still good to go with me to the mine?"

"Absolutely. I'm anxious to learn all I can about mineral exploration in the rainforests. Heck, I might be running my own expedition someday soon."

Dawson had mixed feelings, some joyful – others painful. "What a great opportunity. I'm proud of you. So, we'll fly to the mine, I'll show you around, we'll have a nice dinner and... I've reserved a separate room for you... unless..." Dawson winked and raised a brow, searching for a sign.

"That's very considerate of you." She read his body language but knew she shouldn't make any commitments.

"It's my pleasure. Besides, the more you know about the rainforest, the easier and safer it will be when you're out there on your own."

*****

As the helicopter approached Keystone airport, Teddy made a slow pass over the massive open-pit chasm.

"Oh, my God!" Cece cried out. "I never imagined... this thing is gigantic. I've seen other open-pit mines but never one as big as this. It's incredible. Breathtaking."

"Keystone is the third largest open-pit mine in the world," Dawson said with a pinch of vanity.

"How big is it?" asked Cece.

"Three thousand meters across. Twenty-five truck terraces lead down to the bottom at fifteen hundred feet. This mine is like a giant upside-down pyramid. In fact, you could put a hundred Giza Pyramids inside this pit and still have room for a hundred more. Sorry, we don't have a Starbucks on site."

"Those ore trucks – they're monsters."

"They're the biggest and most powerful in the business. These giants can haul five hundred tons of ore up the slope at sixty klicks per hour."

After circling the mine twice, Teddy settled the helicopter on the tarmac.

"Nice airport, Dawson," said Cece.

"It works for us. Keystone is really a small town. Two thousand employees, five hundred dependents. Single men are housed in a dormitory. Married couples are assigned to one of our village apartments. There's a shopping mall, a few restaurants, day-care center, pre-school through twelfth grade, soccer field, theater and a couple of churches. We even have our own medical center and hospital, free jitney service, security and fire departments. We provide free medical care, bus service to Wabag, Internet and cell phone access. Not exactly LA, but for this part of the world, it's utopia."

"It's the most impressive third world mine I've ever seen. You should be very pleased. Nice work, Dawson. I'm proud to know you." Cece kissed him lightly on the cheek.

"We do our best. Over there, in the hangar, we have a twelve-passenger Lear jet – mostly for company executives and ex-pat rotation, government inspectors and dignitaries. We also have a Piper Aztec for aerial surveys. She's Teddy's favorite – equipped with ground penetrating radar and magnetometers – everything needed to give us a better understanding of what lies below. It's ideal for our Gemini Falls survey. And if by chance the data indicates the presence of any rare earth elements, you're welcome to take it with you. It might come in handy for your meeting next week."

"Thanks, Dawson. What's the survey plan? When will you have the data?"

"Teddy will take us to Gemini Falls tomorrow. I need to check out the geology, retrieve a few samples and take some photos of any promising outcrops."

"And what comes after that?"

"I'll review the data. You can help if you wish. Then, we'll mobilize the site-prep crew and our heavy-lift helicopter. This bird has a winch system and a basket so we can deploy men and equipment while hovering above the rainforest. The site-prep crew will clear-cut a large area for the core drilling operations and set up a campsite. They'll try to clear the area of poisonous snakes, tarantulas, and jumbo centipedes – as many as they can find. They probably won't get them all. There's a thousand ways to die in the rainforest."

"I hate snakes – live ones – dead ones. Either way I get the jitters. We had similar problems in Vietnam – poisonous snakes, thirty-seven species. Fea's Vipers were the deadliest, and the Malayan krait, banded krait, red-headed krait. They're killers."

"Jesus. What are the Vietnamese doing with so many different snakes – raising them for Pho?"

"As a matter of fact, I've eaten snake Pho, snake soup, snake dumplings – even tried a plate of crispy fried snake skins. I probably should take dead snakes off my list of jitter-makers."

"I'm impressed. You've certainly got more courage than I. Come with me. I'll take you to your room, then we can have lunch and I'll show you around the processing and refining areas. Sorry, there's no snake on our menu. But if you wish, we can take a ride to the bottom of the pit in one of my big ore trucks. I guarantee it's more thrilling than a roller coaster."

*****

The next day, as they flew over the rainforest, Cece seemed edgy. It was a muggy morning and she was sweating profusely.

"Are you okay?" Dawson shouted over the noise of the helicopter.

Cece shouted back. "Snakes, tarantulas, and centipedes. I told you. I'm not okay with creepy-crawly things."

"Mike and his crew will kill most of them. Don't worry. You and I will not be venturing too far into the bush. But if you encounter one, just back away and let someone know."

"But what if I get bit?"

"We've brought plenty of anti-venom just in case. Just keep alert and watch where you're going."

After reaching Gemini Falls, Teddy pitched the helicopter upriver until he found a small clearing along the muddy shore. He hovered directly over the area and gently settled on the soggy ground.

"Dawson, how much time do you need?"

"No more than an hour. I need to collect a few rocks along the shore and sort out the best place to drill core samples."

"Great. I'll wait."

"Come on, Cece. Ladies first." Dawson opened the metal barricade and stepped to the ground. "Come, take my hand. Don't be afraid. There not a single snake in sight."

Cece followed.

"That wasn't so bad, was it? Let's go get some rocks," Dawson shouted while retrieving his miner's pick from his belt. "I'll look for the rocks. You keep an eye out for crocodiles."

"Crocodiles! I thought we had to keep an eye out for snakes and bugs?"

"Crocs, my dear, are man-eaters. Snakes and bugs? They might bite, but you won't be turned into croc poop."

The couple navigated along the river's edge until encountering a rocky outcrop blocking their path.

"That's interesting," said Dawson. "Looks epithermal, mafic diorite perhaps."

He smashed his miner's pick across the leading edge of the protruding formation, dislodging a fist-size fragment.

After a close inspection with his 10X eye loupe he smiled, and looked at Cece with a twinkle in his eye.

"Hey, Cece. Look what we have here." Dawson handed her the specimen and his eye loupe. "Do you see what I see?"

Peering through the optics she exclaimed, "Quartz, and... Oh, my God... jade."

"Look a little closer at the dark host material. See those little specks?"

"Oh, yeah! They're everywhere. Is that what I think it is?"

"You got it. Flakes of pure gold. Gold, Cece. And there's likely to be plenty of it right here under our feet. That's damn exciting, eh? Let me knock off a few more samples and we'll get back to the chopper. Teddy will flip out when he hears the news."

Teddy was enjoying the mating ritual of a pair of birds-of-paradise when Dawson and Cece returned. The male was presenting the female with a romantic dance of colorful tail feathers – shape-shifting his distinctive plumage in an amazing display of courtship.

"Take a peek at what we've found." Dawson handed Teddy a canvas backpack filled with rocky samples.

"That didn't take long. Let me guess. You've found another strike." Teddy retrieved a large rock and rotated it under his gaze. "Nice. Very nice. Whaddaya think – twelve, maybe fourteen grams per ton."

"That's what I'm guessing. Alby will let us know after he does his magic. Let's get back to Keystone. I've got to prepare a core-drilling plan."

As they flew back to Keystone, Dawson began to wonder how he might persuade her to stay. Other than his professed love, he really had nothing to offer but a spirited good time in the sack. Knowing how much she wanted to do her own thing, he assumed that would not be enough incentive to change her mind.

"Teddy has scheduled your flight to Port Moresby for nine tomorrow morning. I'm going to miss you, Buttercup."

She didn't hear his words over the noise of the engines, but she read his lips and felt his heartache. She didn't know what to say. She was still playing Rubik's Cube, trying to line up all the colors – searching for a solution to their mutual plight. She believed there was no other option except for her to go about her work and dream that someday, maybe they would meet again under more favorable circumstances.

After returning to Keystone, Dawson lobbied for more of her time. "How about dinner at my place. I make a mean lasagna. We can split a bottle of dago red – maybe take a moonlight dip in the pool."

Cece couldn't prolong their mutual suffering any more than she already had. "That's probably not a good idea. Besides, I'm pooped and need to get a good night's sleep. I'll call you when I find out more about this PNG project. Maybe we can touch base next time you're in the city."

Dawson let his chin drop and sighed. He then kissed her swiftly on the cheek and walked away.

Later that night, when the moon was high and the lights were low, she came to him softly – wearing the libidinous scent of a woman in lust – gifting her body – her spirit, and gentle touch. She was silent in the night, spoke not a single word, just pulled back the sheets and pressed her naked body next to his.

And then she was gone.

CHAPTER FIVE

Hovering a few feet over the clear-cut area, Teddy fought a persistent headwind compelling him to use all his flying skills to maintain his position. Hanging from the underbelly of the heavy-lift helicopter was an expanded metal baseplate designed to support the core drilling system while allowing water and drilling fluids to seep into the ground.

On the ground, the drill crew struggled to keep the awkward load from spinning out of control. Overwhelmed by the dissonance of the twin turbojet engines, they communicated with Teddy using hand signals. A twirling index finger pointed upward meant come up on the load – pointed down signaled the winch operator to lower the load. A closed fist meant stop.

Tony Esperanza was the crew leader. Everyone who knew him called him "Snake." He claimed to be the only man in the world to have survived the bite from three different deadly snakes: a banded krait, a brown taipan, and a death adder. Because of his size and stature, his bragging rights were seldom challenged.

His six-man crew, Tank, Buddy, Chester, Lenny, Willy, and Danny, were indigenous Papuan natives who worked long, hard hours and received twice the income and benefits of the average native.

With the baseplate no longer connected, Teddy landed the helicopter and the crew began offloading the remaining equipment. Snake retrieved his twelve-gauge shotgun, ammo, and satellite phone and then took charge of the offloading sequence.

The coring system was designed and packaged so that two men could unload everything needed in the shortest possible time. The crew came well prepared for a thirty-day operation. Unloading the coring rig, drill pipe, diamond bits, diesel-electric power generator, food, and water took most of the morning, Teddy had to make several trips to complete the delivery of all the core drilling equipment.

"Drag that baseplate over here." Snake used the heel of his right boot to score a line across the rain-soaked ground. "Chester, you and Lenny set up the mast and make sure it works. Willy, you and Danny hook up the generator and string the night lights. I'll check out the tent and provisions."

It was laborious, sweaty work accompanied by a symphony of obscenities. The men had mixed feelings about working in the rainforest during the monsoon season. The downpour would soak their souls and limit their work, but it would also decrease the number of mosquitos and other blood-sucking insects.

"That's perfect," Snake shouted to Tank. "Now hook up the mud pump and make sure we have good flow. I'm glad we're near a river. We'll need the water. It's gonna be a hot hole and we can't afford to lose any diamond bits."

"Yes, sir, Snake. You're the boss," replied Tank.

"Willy, when you and Danny are done stringing the lights, go dig us a deep shit-hole under that big tree." Snake pointed to the tall tree in the far west corner. "Anyone seen the toilet? Goddamnit! Where's the fucking shitter? And the bug spray? These damn mosquitos are a bitch."

By late afternoon, Teddy had delivered the required drill pipe and diesel fuel. His final delivery – three dozen wood pallets – was in many respects the most important, at least for the comfort and wellbeing of the men. Placed inside the tent, over the water-soaked ground and along the route to the drill rig, these pallets insulated the men from the soggy ground and kept their feet dry enough to avoid foot rot.

"That's all for today," shouted Teddy. "Be sure to keep Dawson up to date on your progress. Let him know if you need anything. I'll do my best to deliver it, pronto."

"Thanks, Teddy. We should be making hole tomorrow. Dawson wants the cores delivered to Alby every hundred feet. I'll call you when we're ready for a delivery. We should have the first ten cores – a hundred feet – in two or three days."

Snake and his crew had worked together on numerous projects. His men worked as a team and gave their very best. They trusted him to be fair minded and make good decisions. Tank, Buddy, and Chester took the first shift – noon to midnight. Lenny, Willy, and Danny would relieve them at midnight.

*****

It didn't take long to drill through ten feet of mud and sand in an unconsolidated material and retrieve the drill pipe containing the first core sample. Removing the sample from the drill pipe was a bit tricky. It required a shot of compressed air. Like toothpaste, as the pressure increased, it forced the core sample from the drill pipe and into a V-shaped, aluminum tray. Too much pressure and the core will shoot out like a rocket. Too little, and it will not budge. As the team leader, Snake took charge of the core removal procedure.

"It's all sediment, overburden, mud, sand, pebbles, and decomposed organics. Save it for Dawson. He might find something." Snake was not disappointed. This was typical overburden geology for PNG.

Hard rock formations were seldom found near the surface. "Let's get through this soft shit as fast as possible. Let me know when you hit a rock-solid formation."

The atmosphere at the drill site could be characterized as cautiously optimistic. During their respective shifts, the men did their job with skill and intensity. They seldom complained – even when someone smashed his thumb or received a knock on the head from swinging drill pipe. Spontaneously, the victim naturally shouted profanities for a few agonizing seconds. But the men of PNG were brave and resilient. They usually shook off the incident and returned to their duties as if it never happened.

*****

"Snake!" Buddy shouted. "Wake up. Tank says we've reached hard rock."

"Well, damn, it's about time. How deep are we?"

"Tank says ninety-eight feet."

Snake pushed the mosquito netting back, climbed from his cot, pulled on his rubber boots and rushed from the tent to the drill rig.

"Whatcha got?"

"I think we hit diorite. Won't know for sure until we pull a core. I should have one out in an hour or two."

"Good. Try one of those new diamond core bits. It might be faster, but you'll need to increase the cooling fluid flow rate."

"Will do."

Two hours later, Snake was looking at the first hard rock core sample.

"Yup, that's it – mafic diorite. Looks like it also contains some nephrite. That's a good sign. Whoa! There are some gold flakes too. Nice. The edge looks clean. That's a good bit. Keep using it until it gets too hot or lose penetration. I've got to call Dawson."

Snake dialed Dawson's number, but it took a few seconds to establish a satellite link. "Hey, boss. We've entered a nice diorite formation after pushing through a hundred feet of sediment. The first core looks great. Gold flakes are visible. Looks very much like the early Keystone samples. I'll let you know when we have ten cores ready for delivery to Alby."

"Nice work. I'll tell Teddy to expect your call."

Dawson fell back against his office chair. Like a double shot of high-octane liquor, a burst of sultry excitement raced through his veins. He could taste the exhilaration – the hypnotic intoxication of another gold strike and the making of another glorious chapter in his book of life.

*****

Snake was born and raised in the coastal city of San Sebastian – in the Basque region of Spain – twelve miles south of the French border. Before joining Keystone, the thirty-two-year-old had worked as a drill rig roughneck in Darwin, Australia, and a lumberjack in the rainforests of Indonesia.

While working in the field, he seldom fell into a deep sleep. And he had never owned a pair of pajamas. His job required him to be available twenty-four/seven. He had learned how to grab fifteen minutes of shut-eye whenever and wherever it was possible, and could doze off leaning against a tree, lying on concrete, or sitting on a hardwood log.

While one crew worked the coring rig, the relief crew slept, ate, visited the outhouse, swatted mosquitos, stomped on tarantulas, ate, chopped off the head of a deadly snake, and slept – not always in that order. During their first week of operation the crew had drilled, and Teddy had delivered thirty, ten foot cores to Alby.

*****

It was shortly past midnight when Danny rushed into the tent. Snake was reading a book. "Hey, boss. Lenny say we hit strange rock. Come now."

"Strange rock? What the fuck does he mean? A strange rock. Christ Almighty. Go tell Lenny I'm on my way. I need to get my boots on."

Snake trudged over the mud-caked wood pallets to the drill rig. "What's all this nonsense about a strange rock?"

Lenny appeared perplexed. "We were making good hole through the diorite. At three-sixty, the bit hit something different – an odd formation – like a steel shell or barricade. The bit began to vibrate, and the penetration rate dropped to near zero. The mud got hot too. There's something down there, and I haven't a fucking clue what it is." Lenny was shaking.

"Has this thing, whatever it is, got you spooked?"

Lenny nodded his head. "It's a sign of the spirits – a bad sign. Something bad is going to happen."

"Pull the drill string and try a number ten diamond bit. Reduce rpm to sixty. Set your downhole bit force at ten kilos. Let the diamonds do their job. Kick up the mud flow to twenty liters a minute and call me if something changes."

"Okay, boss. We'll pull this string and put on a new bit." Lenny knew what was expected of him, but being a native, he was not comfortable with the situation.

Snake didn't share the same superstitions as the natives. He grew up in a cosmopolitan world, had a college degree in engineering and had traveled and worked in dozens of countries. Regardless of his background and common-sense beliefs, there was always the possibility, however remote, that the natives had a fifth sense about the spiritual world. After all, they had survived in their spirit-filled world for many thousands of years. He let his thoughts drift back to his studies in the theory of probability at the University of Barcelona. He recalled his professor quoting an ancient axiom. *If the probability of an event is* _not_ *zero, then that event* _will_ *occur sometime in the future.*

*****

Everyone heard it coming – like a freight train rumbling down the tracks. Situated on the Ring of Fire, PNG experienced some of the world's strongest and most devastating earthquakes. In the past hundred years, the island nation had been cursed and crushed by sixty-five earthquakes measuring seven or more on the Richter Scale.

As the ground began to shimmy, the string of lights swayed willy-nilly. From the rainforest, swarms of black bats screeched in panic across the sky. Waves of river water crashed along the shoreline, eroding tons of sand, mud, pebbles, and rocks.

"That was a big fucker. Maybe a six." Snake caught his breath. "Everyone all right?" There was no reply. The natives were used to big quakes. Some believed they were a bad omen. Others argued they foretold the end of days. Regardless, every year, PNG typically receives eight or more earthquakes with a magnitude of six or more. Some call it the rock-n-roll capital of the Pacific.

The monsoon deluge had arrived, drenching the drill site and making everyone's work and life more difficult. To make matters worse, the tent had sprung a few leaks requiring the cots to be relocated into a smaller space. For the next five months, life in the rainforest would be one of sodden misery.

Tanks crew was tending to the drilling operations when Snake approached for a status check.

"How deep are we?"

"Three-sixty, plus."

"No way. Plus, what?"

"A centimeter, maybe two?"

"That's fucking ridiculous. Something must be terribly wrong. Buddy, get me a sample of the cuttings. Shut this fucker down until we can figure out what's going on. Three-sixty. Shit, we should be at least three-eighty."

Buddy opened the hatch to the cooling mud reservoir and scooped up a sample of cutting sludge with a metal cup.

"Here's the sample, boss."

"Thanks, I'll let you know if I find something strange."

Snake returned to the tent to examine the cuttings from the mysterious barrier. He pinched a sample of the material between his thumb and index finger, rolled it around to remove some of the drill mud and expose the cuttings.

"Ouch, son-of-a-bitch!" he shouted. "Damn stuff is sharp." He held his angry finger up to the light. "Looks like metal cuttings from a machine shop." He grabbed a pair of needle-nose pliers and removed the prickly invader from his finger. Taking a small magnet from his toolbox, he swirled it through the muddy fluid. "Well, I'll be damned," he recoiled. "It's iron. *It's meteoric iron.*"

With a mixture of blood and cooling fluid streaming down his finger and a line of iron flakes standing upright on the magnet, he rushed to the drill site.

"Look what I found. It's iron. We're drilling into an iron meteor. I can hardly believe it. It's probably been here at least a hundred million years – maybe five hundred million. There were many meteor impact events in the past. This one probably smashed into earth during the Paleozoic or Mesozoic, when earth was called Pangea – before the continents separated into their current location. Wow! This is an amazing discovery. Dawson will shit a brick." Snake's explanation fell on clueless ears. None of the men in his crew knew what the hell he was talking about.

"Sorry, boss," Tank growled. "I don't understand what this is, how or when it got here or anything about a place called Pangea. All I know is I'm having trouble drilling a hole in it."

"I understand. Relax. Take a break. I've got to call Dawson."

Snake returned to the tent, wiped the rain from his face and the sludge from his hand and called Dawson on his satellite phone.

After four rings, Dawson answered with a drowsy voice. "Hey, Snake. It's four in the morning. What's the problem?"

"We've struck an iron meteor at three-sixty," he bellowed.

There was a pregnant pause. "You're fucking joking?" Dawson took a moment to consider the facts. "You're serious?"

"I'm not joking. I've got the cuttings to prove it – magnetic cuttings. It's meteoric. It came from outer space hundreds of millions of years ago. It's buried in the diorite."

"Holy shit. That's friggin nuts. What do you think we should do?"

"Hell, we're at three-sixty. I want to drill through it. We know the diorite is high-grade ore and the core samples have shown higher readings as we drill deeper. We don't know how big the meteor is so moving to another location and drilling a new hole is risky. I might need more number ten bits, but I'd like to try."

"You're right about the ore body – deeper is better. Alby has assayed our first twenty diorite cores. He's confirmed they were better than Keystone."

"Teddy delivered ten more cores yesterday."

"You're right. I need to contact Alby. In the meantime, keep drilling. What is your spindle speed and downhole bit pressure?"

"Sixty rpm. Ten kilos."

"That's too fast. Reduce your rpm to forty. Keep the same bit pressure. I'll get you some better bits. Damn! Now I've got to get up. I couldn't go back to sleep if you drugged me."

*****

"Snake!" Willy screamed running into the tent. "We broke through the iron. Lenny says we're back drilling into diorite, same as before. Come, see."

Willy led the way, running toward the drill rig. Snake followed at a jog across the pallet walkway.

"What's your depth?" Snake inquired.

"Three-sixty-eight. But… but."

"But, what?"

"The bottom of the iron formation fell out at three-sixty plus two inches." replied Lenny.

"What do you mean, the bottom fell out?"

"There was nothing there. The bit dropped six feet in less than a minute. It felt like drilling through sweet potatoes. At three sixty-six, we were back drilling into the iron again. Then at three-sixty-six plus two inches, we were drilling in diorite. There's something alien down there and… *I'm fucking scared.*"

"Don't be afraid, Lenny. God didn't make this world to scare humans. There are lots of things we don't know or understand. Your spirits might be wrong. Look around you. What do you see? Rainforest, animals, birds, insects. They've been here for millions of years. If there was something alien, something bad living deep in the earth, these animals would not be living here. If there is something down there, it won't hurt you. It's just another type of dirt, only tougher."

"Okay, if you say so. But I warned you."

*****

Like sharing a cigarette or a bottle of water, the crew changes became routine. Tank and his crew ate an early lunch and had arrived at the drill rig on time to relieve Lenny and his crew. Snake was there to brief them.

"We had an interesting night. Lenny struck an iron meteor, drilled through it, and has a core sample ready for recovery. So, let's get to it. Pull the string and let's see what we've got."

Ninety minutes later, Tank and Chester entered the tent and laid the core tube on the extraction table. Everybody gathered in a semi-circle, anxious to see the strange core. Unable or unwilling to contravene his superstitions, Lenny stood well back from the core.

Snake connected the pneumatic hose and opened the valve. Nothing happened. He increased the air pressure. Still nothing happened.

"It must be plugged. Stand back. I'm going to blow this fucker out." He increased the pressure to the maximum and the core shot out like a fastball.

Everyone stood in awe. The core was divided into five discrete sections. The first two feet were distinctly diorite, followed by a two-inch section of greyish metal. A six-foot section of what looked like black petrified wood occupied the middle of the core, followed by another two-inch section of iron and two more feet of diorite.

Snake was intrigued. He was certain the metal was meteoric iron. But he was completely dumbfounded as to the composition of the mysterious black material. He picked up a screwdriver and stabbed the strange substance. A couple of small chips broke away, bounced off the wooden pallet with a dull thunk, and tumbled unnoticed into the soggy ground.

"I've never seen anything like this. It might be petrified organic material – like petrified wood. But these meteoric iron sections above and below really have me stumped. I've read about iron meteors. Geologists find them all over the planet. But how this darker material found its way inside a meteor is beyond my comprehension. Maybe it's another type of rock, or a mixture of other elements. I'm truly baffled. Teddy arrives tomorrow to pick up a load of cores for Alby. He'll be shocked when he sees this one. Okay, the show is over. Back to work. Let's make some hole."

*****

It had rained all night and was still pouring when Teddy circled the campsite. The whine from the twin turbojets meshing with the thump-thump beat of the twin rotors announced his arrival. The monsoon rains were in full force. The Lagaip river had risen to near flood state while its boiling current continued to rip large sections of sand, mud, and undergrowth from the riverbank.

He settled the helicopter onto the spongy ground and opened the cargo bay door. Dawson stood in the opening while two Keystone mine workers jumped to the ground.

Snake rushed to greet them. "The cores are in the tent," he shouted. "They're all marked with the date and depth. Dawson, you gotta see core three sixty-seven. It's the most amazing thing I've ever encountered. I think it's an iron meteor. But there's something in the middle that is incomprehensible. Come inside. Let's get out of this downpour."

Dawson jumped to the ground and slogged his way into the tent while being drenched by the unrelenting torrent. Teddy remained in the cockpit.

Dawson and Snake wiped the water from their faces as they approached the core extraction table. "There it is," proclaimed Snake pointing to the sixth core in the lot.

Awestruck, Dawson stopped in his tracks. "What in the bloody hell is that black shit in the middle?" he marveled. "Looks like petrified wood."

"That's what I thought too. I thought you'd find this... interesting."

"Interesting? This is much more than interesting. This thing is... implausible... enigmatic. I don't know if there is a word that adequately describes this... *thing.*"

Dawson fixed his eyes on the black material, laced his fingers together, and reached back to his days at Caltech.

"I agree these metallic sections look like meteoric iron. You did test for magnetism?"

"Oh, yeah, it's definitely magnetic," Snake held up his shop magnet bearing flakes of iron.

"So, this iron meteor impacted the earth – maybe billions of years ago – and over time, it became buried under hundreds of feet of volcanic rock and sediment until you just accidentally drilled a hole in it."

"Yup. That's how I see it."

"Unfuckingbelievable! Alby will shit a cassowary egg when he sees this – maybe two cassowary eggs. Let's get these cores on the chopper. Alby's men will meet us when we arrive."

"Come on, guys. Load these cores in the chopper. Be careful. Don't drop any," barked Snake. "That's it. That's the last one – the one with the unknown shit in the middle."

"I wish we had more time to talk, but I need to be going. You and your men are doing a great job. I know it's tough out here with this rain, but it will be worth it if we find another deposit like Keystone. I'll discuss this more-than-interesting core with Alby. Call me if you need anything."

"Thanks, Dawson. I'll keep you informed."

*****

It was still raining when the Keystone helicopter arrived in Wabag. Alby's men were waiting. They quickly loaded the cores into the back of their F-250 extended-cab four-wheel pick-up and delivered them to Alby's assay facility.

Wabag was located about fifty miles southeast of the Keystone mine. It was once a town of hooligans and thieves. Roving gangs repeatedly broke into shops and government offices, stealing anything of value and burning what was left. They even ransacked the public library, stole the books and used the pages to roll cigarettes. Tribal infighting was more of a sporting event. Spectators came from remote villages to bet on their favorites. After years of neglect, the government stationed a company of Military Police to restore law and order.

At an elevation of six thousand feet, Wabag is a modern highland outpost with a population of about five thousand people. Most of the men are truck drivers or work for Keystone.

Alby was standing in front of his building to meet them. "Hey, Dawson. Good to see you. I guess that Smaark fellow put you onto a hot spot. The diorite is looking very promising. Where's your lady friend – Suzy Dream Queen? Sorry, I mean Cece. She's a bit of all right, mate," Alby chuckled, pumping his fist.

"She's under contract to conduct an exploration project for the PNG government. I don't think she'll be back anytime soon. We're pleased with the core samples. But I've got something to show you that will blow your friggin mind."

"As long as I don't lose my head, let's take a look."

In a room filled with hundreds of samples, the most recent cores were easily recognized – they were dripping wet.

"Check out core three sixty-seven," urged Dawson.

"Holy crocodiles! What the flyin fuck is this. Wait just a second. You've salted this core with a piece of charcoal? You can't fool me. No, siree. I'm nobody's fool."

"This is serious, Alby. Snake cored this from the diorite formation at a depth of three hundred and sixty-eight feet."

Alby gave Dawson a dubious eye. "Okay, I'll look at it later. It's past five and I'm thirsty. Time for a cold one. It's happy hour. I'm buyin. Lulu's is just around the corner."

*****

The monsoon rains continued with little reprieve, making it difficult for the drill crews to make hole at the desired rate. As their progress degraded, everyone realized they would be spending more time on this job in the rainforest than anticipated. It soon became a blame game – one crew against the other. Tempers flared at the slightest provocation. Arguments over minuscule issues led to pushing and shoving. Lenny's crew came to loathe Tank's crew – and the feeling was mutual. Snake tried to keep order while doing everything possible to complete his assignment. Nevertheless, core drilling was significantly compromised by the foul weather and heated temperament.

Tank's crew had drilled to a depth of about four hundred and fifty feet and were in the process of retrieving a core when the generator suddenly died.

"Damn it. We're fucked!" screamed Tank, looking up at the downpour. "Chester, come with me. Help me check out the fucking generator. There's not much daylight left."

Snake was accustomed to the noise of the equipment. So, when the diesel-electric generator stopped, he instinctively knew something was wrong. He rushed from the tent, hopped and skipped from pallet to pallet toward the drill rig. "Tank, what's with the generator?" he shouted.

"I'm working on it. I think it's the rain – got to the alternator – battery won't charge. I can smell it – shorted out. This piece of shit is dead. You better call for a replacement and a new battery too."

"Okay, make sure we've got plenty of flashlights. We'll be in the dark until the chopper can deliver a new unit and we get it up and running. Secure the rig as best you can. We'll resume as soon as we get power."

Snake returned to the tent and reached for his satellite phone. Dawson answered on the third ring.

"Hello, Tony. What's up?" Dawson occasionally called Snake by his given name.

"The generator crapped out. We don't have power. We're dead until we get a replacement."

"Damnit!" Exasperated, Dawson took a deep breath.

"We might have one here. What are the specs?"

"Two-forty – twenty-five kW. My sat. phone is low on juice and I have no way to recharge it until we get another generator."

"I'll do my best. You better figure on being without power until tomorrow morning. I hope you guys brought your flashlights."

"Yeah, we've got extra batteries, too."

*****

The sun had burned off the morning mist when Lenny returned from a routine visit to the outhouse. The rain was taking a break and the cloud cover had broken up. He grabbed a cup of hot coffee and walked toward the exit. As he passed the core extraction table, something caught his attention. Curious, he approached the strange reflection and bent over for a closer look.

"Mushrooms," he mumbled. After gazing at the cluster, he reached down and touched one of the conical caps. It instantly quivered and expelled a puff of white powder into his face, burning his eyes and causing him to grimace in pain.

"Damn!" he shouted, spilling his coffee. Tears quickly filled his angry eyes. A peppery aroma washed across his nose triggering a trio of violent sneezes. He stood upright, shook his head, and waited for the effects to wear off.

After a few minutes, his senses returned to near normal and he continued his scrutiny of the mushroom cluster. There were about a dozen fresh-looking sprouts – many about the same size as his thumb. Atop each stem was a bright red cap about the size of a golf ball. Each one was adorned with an array of pearl-white dots – like an artist had painted them with a fine-bristled brush.

Being a native of PNG, Lenny was quite familiar with mushrooms. He knew which ones were edible, those that were psychedelic, and the ones that would kill you if you were sufficiently mentally impaired or suicidal to eat one. Lenny had never seen any mushrooms like these.

Standing on the wooden walkway, Tank and Buddy were drinking coffee and chatting when Lenny approached a short time after his encounter with the weird mushrooms.

"Afternoon," said Buddy. "Nice day, eh?"

"Yeah, it sure beats the rain. Hey, did either of you see those strange-looking mushrooms growing under the extraction table?" Tank and Buddy looked at each other and shrugged their shoulders. Neither seemed interested.

"They're bright red with white spots. One of them squirted some white powdery shit all over my face. It stung my eyes and caused me to sneeze. I've never seen them before. They smelled like pepper too."

"Hey, guys," Snake interrupted. "I just talked to the boss. Teddy is on his way with another generator. We'll be back in business soon."

*****

It was nearing the midnight crew change when Lenny awoke with a raging headache. His body ached from head to toe. He tried to stretch his arms and legs, but every muscle seemed locked in concrete. Knowing his crew depended on him, he struggled to his feet and immediately collapsed onto the pallet flooring.

"Hey, man!" Willy bellowed. "Are you sick?"

"I don't feel good. I'm stiff as bamboo and dizzy. I'll shake it off," Lenny coughed.

"Holy pek-pek. Your eyes are bloody. Lay back on your cot."

Willy ran outside shouting, "Snake, Lenny is sick. His eyes are red. Come quick."

As he lay on his cot, Lenny began to shiver. An overwhelming tickling sensation grew in his throat. He felt like he was being strangled. Moments later he disgorged a bloody mass into his cupped hands. The sight of his blood terrified him, and he quickly swiped the blood-stained goop onto the pallet flooring. Moments later, an avalanche of vertigo crushed his equilibrium. Waves of nausea raced through his stomach. He leaned forward and vomited. Shocked at the sight of more blood and a white, thread-like substance, he emitted a deep moan.

"Lenny, talk to me. Tell me where it hurts. Were you bitten by a death adder?" Snake asked.

Lenny shook his head and mumbled, "No."

"A tarantula? A centipede? Damn, you're burning up. Your face is bright red. You need to see a doctor."

"No, no." Lenny shook his head. "I'll be okay. Just let me sleep. I'll feel better tomorrow."

"Okay, but if you're not better, I'm calling for the chopper."

"Just give me some time. I'll be better tomorrow."

Snake turned to his men. "Shut everything down. Let's take a break. We'll resume operations tomorrow if Lenny is okay. If not, we'll get a replacement."

*****

Lenny lay in a lethargic stupor, progressively drawn deeper into an apparition. His mental visions drifted back to his childhood days, living in the sanctum of his highland village. His face quivered and twitched as fragments of his earliest memories floated across his semi-conscious cerebral cortex.

It was a time of celebration. Village men danced and chanted to the monotonic beat of slit sago drums. Shortly, the ghostly image of his father glided through the blackness, his cheeks caked with red and yellow mud – a cassowary claw thrust through his nose – crescent-shaped kina shells dangling from his earlobes. A string of crocodile teeth encircled his slender neck, signifying his regal stature among his people. Cupped in his hands rested a human skull, a symbol of power and potency. As his father edged closer to his face, he suddenly perceived himself helplessly trapped inside the human skull – his skull.

In a flash, he was airborne, soaring above the mighty Sepik river – surrounded by a swarm of stinging mosquitos – watching his father paddle his canoe – hunting for crocodiles with a bow and arrow – chewing betelnut – chanting to the *yalyakali*, the sky people – beseeching them for good luck and protection from the *pututuli*, cannibalistic, shape-changing demons who lived in the rainforest. A thick mist appeared before him, its smoky white haze slowly swallowing his father and his canoe.

Instantly transported to another place and time, he was now facing his wife, Kyt, holding her hand, rubbing his thumb in the valley of her palm. She was crying. It was camouflaged under a scattering of dead broadleaf ferns – she never saw the death adder before her right foot invaded its domain. The bite was instantaneous – long fangs penetrated deep into her ankle. The neurotoxin raced through her heart and into her central nervous system. Hers was a particularly painful death. At first, she screamed, *"It hurts so bad!"* An hour later, she yelled, *"I don't want to die!"* When the pain became too much to bear, she begged, *"Kill me. Kill me now!"* The moment she took her last breath, a colony of giant black bats swooped down from above, snapping their devilish fangs and swatting him unmercifully with their massive wings.

Strangely, he was now awake – magically energized – determined to complete a new mission. His breathing was labored, barely able to sustain life. From his throat came a wheezing, crackling sound accompanying each breath. He felt disconnected from reality. Something inside of him had taken control of his thoughts and actions – compelling him to comply with irrational directives.

He rose upright, the pain in his arms and legs no longer evident. Barefooted, he shuffled across the pallet floor and into the darkness of an overcast night. A light rain sprinkled his face – drops of water drizzled from the tip of his nose. He waddled across the boggy grounds toward the dense line of trees marking the edge of the rainforest. Driven by an invisible authoritarian force, he approached a large, southern beech – its branches swaying willy-nilly in the midnight breeze. He looked up to the top of the majestic giant. A reverent smile grew across his lips. He dropped to his knees at the base of the heavy trunk and began to dig a hole in the rain-soaked mud with his bare hands. As he scooped each handful, a rush of euphoria shot up his spine foretelling an omen that he was going home. After several scoops, he pushed his fingers deep into the hole, cupped a large glob of mud and solemnly smeared it over his face. He laughed fiendishly, and then buried his face in the shallow depression. He was almost home.

*****

Dawson was awakened from an agitated sleep. He had a restless feeling there was something wrong at the core drilling site. It was a subtle, but nevertheless troubling psychotropic sensation. Unable to sleep, he got out of bed, walked to the kitchen and poured himself a glass of cold mango juice. It was a muggy monsoon night. It was not raining, but the forecast was for darkening skies and heavy precipitation for the next several days.

He walked out to his covered lanai and seated himself on a chaise longue. The scotch enabled him to fantasize on the prospects of discovering a gold deposit bigger and more profitable than Keystone. At his age, it was time to start thinking about retirement. Another big strike would do the trick. Dawson flinched as a bolt of lightning flashed down from thunderclouds roaring in from the west. He mentally counted the time between the flash and the bang.

"Hmm, thirty seconds, six miles, give or take." The rumblings triggered his curiosity. "I wonder what's happening at the drill site. Haven't heard from Snake in several days. He would have called if there was a problem."

The sudden ring of his phone brought him back from his imaginings. Dawson looked at his watch. It was five-thirty in the morning. He answered on the third ring.

"Hello, Snake. What's up?" The pause was too protracted to portend good news. "Talk to me," he bellowed.

"Lenny is dead."

"My God. That's terrible. I had no idea he was sick. What happened?"

"We found his body near the trees. It's looks like – he somehow – oh, fuck, Dawson." Snake choked up. "I can't explain it. I have no idea how this happened. I found him kneeling, face down. When I turned him over, there were mushrooms growing from his mouth and nose. It was the most gruesome thing I've ever seen – and I've seen some fuckin awful shit."

"Goddamnit. I'm so sorry. He was a good man, a spiritual man. He held fast to his native beliefs. Are you okay? How are the other men dealing with this?"

"Yeah," Snake sighed. "I'm okay, but my men are not taking this well. They're native Papuans and very superstitious. What's weird about this – Lenny predicted something would go wrong when we recovered the iron meteor core. I thought it was just a silly prophecy, something he heard from the elders about an evil Papuan spirit."

"Mushrooms? That's crazy. Mushrooms don't grow inside humans." Bewildered, Dawson shook his head. "Where's his body?"

"No one wanted to go anywhere near it. I tossed a blanket over him and called you. You better get someone up here immediately – take his body to Wabag."

"Okay, I'll call Teddy and the authorities in Wabag. I know this is upsetting to you and everyone else. Please give the men my best and let them know Lenny will receive an honorable burial. I promise."

"Thanks, Dawson. Talk to you later."

Dawson was a practical man with more than thirty years of field experience, much of it in PNG. He had learned a great deal about the native people. He respected their customs and Christian beliefs and did his best to care for them and their families.

After reporting Lenny's death to the Wabag medical examiner and police, he called Alby to advise him the Gemini Falls gold exploration operations were temporarily on hold.

Alby's phone rang four times before the recorded voice greeted him. Dawson left a message. "Hey, Alby. It's Dawson. Call me as soon as you get this message. I've got some disappointing news."

*****

From Gemini Falls, Teddy turned the helicopter northwest, then followed the river until reaching the drilling site. The Lagaip river defined the southern border of the campsite while the rainforest marked the east, west, and northern boundaries. The core drilling rig, mud pump, and diesel-electric power generator were centered in the northern quadrant. The large personnel tent was centered in the south quadrant. Initially, the campsite grounds were clear-cut, leaving only a couple of inches of wild grasses, weeds, and other vegetation. Since then, the vegetation had grown to about eight inches thick and had penetrated through the wooden pallet walkway. Short stalks of wild shrubs and vines grew even higher, making the campsite appear more like an abandoned homestead than an active drill site.

Thirty-nine-year-old Doctor Paz Cota was one of four Keystone physicians. He was a shy, soft spoken native Papuan with short black hair and big brown eyes. He specialized in internal medicine and respiratory infections – the most common ailments suffered by the Keystone mine workers and their resident dependents. He was born in Port Moresby. His father was a wealthy landowner and member of the PNG parliament. As the eldest son, he grew up in a world of power, prestige, and privilege. He wasn't the sharpest medical student, but with a sizeable endowment from Papa he was able to graduate from Port Moresby Medical University and claim an internship at the Keystone medical center. Here, he quickly earned a reputation as a man of few words and who was often mistaken.

So, when he was assigned to recover Lenny's body, he jumped at the opportunity to showcase his medical prowess and prove he was worthy of his position to his peers and critics. He chose two nurses to join him, nursing specialist Lisa Manka and Johnny Tanso. The possibility that he and his team would be exposed to a biohazard never crossed his mind. *Why should it?*

Lisa Manka was his most trusted assistant. She was thirty-three, shorter and thicker than most Papuan women, with short black hair and alert brown eyes. She was the portrait of a no-nonsense caregiver and a stickler for sanitary protocol.

Johnny Tanso was twenty-two years old. Although he was young, his medical skills and knowledge of poisonous snakes were more advanced than most of his peers'.

*****

Teddy positioned the helicopter away from the sun's glare, descended to about one hundred feet, and hovered over the drill site for a few moments while the medical team prepared to exit. When the chopper settled to the ground, Teddy cut the engines and opened the cabin door. It was a typical muggy day and the medical team quickly broke into an irksome sweat.

Snake greeted the medical team. "Welcome, Doctor. As you can see, it's not the most luxurious place but it's home for us. I see you've brought some company."

"Yes, my nurses, Lisa and Johnny. They'll be assisting. Please take us to the body?"

"Certainly. Follow me."

Cota pulled on a pair of rubber gloves, then gingerly pulled back the blanket exposing Lenny's corpse.

"Oh! No!" Lisa cupped her hand over her mouth and began to hyperventilate. Pursing her lips, she inhaled and exhaled several deep breaths. Shortly, her respiration returned to near normal, but her face held the embodiment of terror – like this was her first encounter with a real ghoul.

"Holy shit," blurted Johnny. "There's mushrooms growing out of his mouth and nose. They're all over his face."

"Are you okay?" Cota asked Johnny.

"I'm fine. I've seen many dead people, some a lot worse, crocodile and snakebite victims mostly. But this is much more… revolting."

The medical team was puzzled by the mushrooms. Out of curiosity, Doctor Cota pinched one of the stems. A burst of white spores flashed into his face. He gasped and instantly lurched back, rubbing his burning eyes. His nose twitched, triggering a barrage of sneezes.

Cota wiped his tearing eyes. "I think I made a mistake. I'm sorry, so sorry. God forgive me," he mumbled.

"What's wrong, Doctor?" asked Snake.

"Nothing. Let's get the corpse in a body bag and aboard the helicopter. The Wabag medical examiner is expecting us."

"My men won't go near the corpse, so I guess you, me, and Johnny will have to do the heavy lifting."

"No. You stay back. Johnny and I can manage."

After loading the body on the helicopter, Doctor Cato entered the cockpit.

"Teddy, I need to call the Wabag medical examiner. Can I use your phone?"

"Sure. Have a seat. It's in the side compartment."

The call was quickly answered.

"Hello, Paz. Is everything okay? We're expecting you. When will you arrive?"

"We've just picked up the body I told you about. We expect to arrive at the heliport in about thirty minutes. I have reason to believe his death was due to a biological infection – possibly related to mushrooms. I had contact with the body, but there was no blood or body fluids. But to be safe, I strongly recommend your people wear level-four PPE and follow the appropriate CDC protocols."

"I understand. Are you sure it's not a snake bite, dengue, or malaria? Some strains can be difficult to diagnose."

"Not likely. We recovered the body in the rainforest. I really don't know how he died. You may need to contact the CDC. They may have some information in their database."

"Good idea. Our ambulance will meet you at the airport when you land."

*****

Dawson had just finished his evening meal when his phone rang.

"Hi, Snake. What's happening?"

"My men are sick – same symptoms as Lenny. They can't get out of bed – coughing and wheezing. Willy and Danny are worse. Their eyes are bloodshot, they're dizzy and coughing up blood."

"How about you? Your voice is raspy."

"I've had a few sneezing and coughing spells. It feels like a respiratory infection. We need to get out of here. There's something evil in this place. I think it's the mushrooms."

"No way. Mushrooms are not dangerous unless you eat a poisonous species."

"But that might be how Lenny died. Christ, Dawson, they were growing out of his mouth and nose. Maybe we'll all die that way."

"Bullshit. You're still alive. It's probably the flu. It's seasonal and now is the season."

"We need to get out of here, now. Send the chopper now!"

"Okay. Stay calm. Teddy will fly up there as soon as possible."

*****

The following morning, Dawson answered his smartphone on the first ring. "Hi, Teddy. How's Snake and the rest of the team?"

"I've got Snake. He's having difficulty breathing and needs medical attention. We're on our way back to Keystone. That's the good news." Teddy swallowed hard.

"So, what's up with the others – the crew?"

Teddy sputtered. "They're... *they're all dead!*"

"What! That's crazy. First Lenny, now five more. This is devastating. I've never heard of such a thing. Goddamn." Dawson took a deep, remorseful breath and exhaled through pursed lips.

"It was very gruesome. There was no way I could recover the bodies. It looks like they committed suicide. Let me tell ya, Dawson, there's something insane going on up there. Fucking mushrooms were growing out of their mouth and nose – just like Lenny. You need to call the medical examiner – get them involved. When we delivered Lenny to the Wabag ME, Cato told him this might be a biohazard problem. I now believe he was right."

"How in the hell could it be a biological hazard? It could have been a snakebite, or some other poisonous critter, or maybe a type of virus. I don't know. Damnit."

"Dawson, listen to me. If Cato is right and it is a biological hazard, the Wabag ME or some other qualified authority should recover the bodies. I'm not hauling any more infected corpses – it's not in my job description."

"Biohazard! Fuck! They'll probably quarantine the operation. We won't be able to recover more core samples. Fuckin bureaucrats."

"I'm about to land. Please have an ambulance meet me. We need to get Snake to the clinic."

"Okay, Teddy. I'll call Wabag and tell them to recover the bodies."

Immediately after hanging up the phone, Dawson called the Keystone medical clinic and asked to speak with Doctor Kennedy.

"Hey, Doc, it's Dawson. We've got a sick man arriving by helicopter. I need you to send an ambulance to pick him up. It's Tony Esperanza – some sort of respiratory issue. Did Cota tell you he thought Lenny's death might be related to a biohazard incident?"

"Yes. I thought he was pulling my leg. Then I thought he might be confused or maybe ate some of those psychedelic shrooms he discovered." Kennedy chuckled. "I'm not aware of any mushrooms that grow inside humans. But I will issue a biohazard warning to my staff. Anyone with mushrooms growing out of their mouth and nose will be stopped, frisked, and isolated in a padded cell." Incredulous, Kennedy tried to marginalize the biological hazard thesis. "Sorry, I apologize for being flippant. Seriously, we don't have any level-four capabilities and very little PPE for a biohazard situation."

"It's not funny, Doctor. Cato may be spot on. Teddy just advised me that five of my men are dead with mushrooms sprouting from their mouth and nose. I'm going to call Wabag ME and have them recover the bodies."

"I really am sorry for my comments. Shame on me. I'm embarrassed. Sorry, I didn't mean to make a joke out of it. You're serious. What about Tony... er Snake?"

"He's having trouble breathing, but there is no evidence of any mushrooms. You may want to put him in ICU until he recovers. If he shows any signs of... you know... call me and the Wabag ME immediately."

"Absolutely."

"Is Cota available? I'd like to speak with him."

"I believe he took a few days off. He seemed stressed."

*****

Dawson walked into the Keystone medical clinic and approached the receptionist.

"I'd like to see Tony Esperanza."

"He's in ICU. It's down the hall to your right. You'll see the sign."

Dawson walked down the long hallway to the ICU, pushed the electronic door activation button and entered the dressing room. He put on a disposable gown, booties, head covering and mask. To his right there were four private ICU rooms. Tony was recovering in unit number one.

"Hello, Mr. Elliott," said the attending nurse.

"Hello, Patricia. How's he doing?"

"He's stable – still on the ventilator though. We've tried several drugs with some improvement. The most effective were the latest antifungals, polyene and echinocandin."

"That is good news. It looks like he's sleeping. I'll come back tomorrow."

"I'm sure he'll be happy to see you."

*****

Placing his first cup of hot coffee on his desk, Dawson seated himself and answered his phone.

"Mr. Elliott?"

"Yes."

"This is homicide detective Victor Santz. One of my officers retrieved a voice message you left for Alby Knight a couple of days ago. Is that correct?"

"Yes, I wanted to tell him about our coring schedule. Is there anything I should know?"

"I'm sorry to tell you this, but Mr. Knight is dead."

"My God! I'm sorry to hear that. He was a good friend and business associate. How did he die? Heart attack? Stroke? He was a party animal, you know."

"The medical examiner has the details, but it appears he suffocated. He found mushrooms growing inside his lungs."

"Mushrooms! Not again. Holy shit. I don't understand. I can't believe he's dead. It's just too bizarre." Dawson took a moment to deliberate the loss of Alby. "Six of my men are dead. We delivered one corpse to the Wabag medical examiner. I assume he's in their morgue. Five bodies are still in the rainforest. I asked the Wabag ME to recover them. He knows about the mushrooms. He said he would discuss it with his superiors and get back to me. Only one man is still alive." Dawson struggled to hold back his tears.

"Yes, we have one corpse in the morgue. Your Doctor Cato called it in. He said it was a biohazard case. We're waiting for the autopsy report. But that is not the entire story," replied Detective Santz.

"There's more?"

"The bodies of Mr. Knight's two assistants were found in his facility – inside the core storage area. Mushrooms were sprouting from their mouth and nose. The same ones that killed Mr. Knight and your man Lenny. I assume you know about that. Do you have any idea how Mr. Knight and his men may have been infected by these mushrooms?"

"No, I really don't. Alby was a good friend. And his men were honest, hard-working Papuans. We've been sending our core samples to him for years. I'm not a biologist, and I don't know of any mushrooms that grow inside humans. It gives me the creeps thinking about it. We did have one core sample that contained some strange material. It was labeled three sixty-seven. Maybe it was something biological. I don't know."

"Some people from the Center for Disease Control conducted an inspection of Mr. Knight's facility. They sealed your cores in hermetic containers and took them to their laboratory in Port Moresby. I just now got off the phone with them. The CDC has determined the deadly mushrooms came from one of your cores – the one you delivered to Mr. Knight – the one you just mentioned."

"I don't know what to say. It is so bizarre. How could any biological organism survive inside an iron meteor for billions of years? That's impossible."

*****

Early the following morning, a neighbor found Doctor Paz Cota's body in his front yard – bent over at the waist – his face covered in mud and mushrooms exploding from his mouth and nose.

Later a security guard found the bodies of nurses Lisa Manka and Johnny Tanso behind their apartment building. They were holding hands – side by side. Their faces were smeared with mud and mushrooms were growing from their mouth and nose.

Just after sunset, a security guard discovered the corpse of Teddy Mitchell in a floodwater drainage ditch. His face was covered with grey mud. Several mushrooms were sprouting from his mouth and nose.

Nothing could have prepared Dawson for the emotional torment he endured after learning of the death of so many good friends and associates. These were men and women who worked for him, trusted him, admired and loved him. Now they were gone, taken by something he could not comprehend or rationalize. He believed these poor souls must have suffered great pain, both physical and mental. Their mysterious death was so outrageous, so egregious, that most people would not have believed it was possible. It was the most depressing and stressful time of his entire life. Every time he thought of how they died, he lost control of his emotions, found a secluded space to bury his face in his hands and sob.

For Dawson, the mental image of spores coming to earth from some other time and space – flourishing in the victim's lungs – sprouting flowering mushrooms from their mouth and nose – spreading their evil offspring to others – was mortifying. And if by chance the outside world heard of such a sordid fable, they would likely believe it was a sickening plot from a low-budget monster movie.

Dawson tumbled into a tunnel of guilt and self-loathing. The scotch he thought would numb the grief didn't do its job. Nothing would bring them back – not prayers – not science – not mystical sorcery. He thought he'd go insane if he couldn't shake the images and dysphoric thoughts from his mind.

Believing he would feel better if he could recall the experience and his feelings on a piece of paper, he drank what was left of his scotch, grabbed a pen and notepad, and began to write his feelings and nightmare accounts of this outrageous saga.

CHAPTER SIX

Three black, unmarked S-92 Sikorski helicopters circled the Keystone airport drawing an audience of curious spectators.

Hearing the roar of the turbojets, Dawson looked out his office window. There was little doubt something of enormous proportions was about to transpire. He broke off his conversation with JoJo, jumped in his four-wheeler, and raced to the Keystone airport terminal. By the time he pulled into his private parking slot, three platoons of uniformed personnel were standing at ease in front of their respective aircraft.

With his heart pounding, Dawson exited his vehicle and walked toward the visitors. Dressed in civilian attire, the apparent leader and two others briskly approached. Like a gunfight scene from an old Western, the principals strutted at an even pace until they were a few feet from Dawson.

"Welcome to Keystone. I'm Dawson Elliott, Managing Director," he proclaimed.

"I'm Doctor Rachel Hemmingway, Head of Mycotic Investigations for the CDC. To my right is Doctor Phillip Jenkins, Chief Scientist with our Pandemic Division. And this is Doctor Quinn McDermott, she's the Principal Investigator for the Invasive Species Group at NASA. May we go somewhere private? We have much to discuss."

Indeed, Dawson was intimidated by the grandiose display of power and authority. Having never experienced this level of pretentious behavior, his mouth became dry.

"It's a pleasure to meet you. I'm sorry I am unprepared, but who are all these people in uniform?" Dawson nodded in the direction of the helicopters.

"That's my security and recovery team – contractors for the CDC. We must speak with you in private."

"Sure. Well, if you don't mind riding in a four-wheeler, I'll drive you and your colleagues to my office. It's not far."

"That will be fine."

Arriving at his office, Dawson escorted his visitors through the lobby, past his office, and into the conference room.

"Would anyone like a cup of coffee, or water?"

"No, thank you." There was no radiance in Rachel's persona. Her blunt, overbearing demeanor made Dawson feel uncomfortably superficial.

Dawson sat at the head of the table. To his thinking, this gave him a slight advantage when it came to negotiations and policy debates. He had reservations as to how effective it would be under these circumstances.

Doctor Hemmingway folded her hands upon the table and gave Dawson an unwavering stare.

"We know about your mushroom problems – and we're here to fix them before they become out of control," she blurted. "Do you have any idea how many people have died due to your... negligence? Don't answer. I'll tell you. First it was Lenny. Then Alby, your assayer and two of his men followed by Dr. Cota, his two nurses, and your chief pilot Teddy Mitchell. Additionally, there are five men whose remains are rotting in the rainforest. Do the math," Hemmingway growled.

Dawson held mixed emotions, but the fire in his belly wasn't about to go unheard. "Listen, Dr. Rachel Herringbone... er, Hemmingway. I've been in the mining business for over thirty years. Do you have any idea how many men have died under my watch? Don't answer. No, you don't, and it's too long a list to recite. Do you have any idea how much it pains me when one of my men or women dies on, or off, the job? No, you obviously don't. Open-pit mining in third world countries is not exactly a walk in the park. It's probably the most dangerous profession on the planet. Accidents happen almost daily. Life-threatening injuries are common occurrences. There's two thousand men here, working twelve-hour shifts. Shit happens! Get it. And while I mourn their deaths, there is nothing you or I or our Heavenly Father can do to change that. Shit happens. Furthermore, Keystone mine has the most stringent safety standards and by far the best safety record of any other open-pit mine in the world. So, with all due respect, Doctor Rachel Hemmingway, don't preach your holier-than-thou bullshit to me." Dawson paused to catch his breath, then took a more constructive approach.

"It all happened too fast. None of us had any idea what it was or where it was heading. At first, most everyone thought it might be a snake bite, or a flu bug. They all died so quickly. I did what I thought was right with the resources we had." Dawson fought to hold back the puddling in his eyes. "I learned about Alby a couple of days ago. He was my best friend." Dawson finished his diatribe with an imperious glower.

"I understand you did what you could. But you can see how fast, and how undeniably fatal this problem has become. No one is blaming you personally. My job is to fix the problem and we need your help to do just that. So please, let's get down to business. Okay?"

"Sure, I'll do what I can to help. You can count on me and my staff." Dawson straightened his back. The look of determination and resolve washed across his face.

Rachel spoke confidently. "Our first mission is to retrieve the five bodies that remain at the Gemini Falls drill site and those of Teddy Mitchell, Doctor Cato and his two nurses. Their corpses will be packaged in accordance with CDC protocols and taken to our research center in Port Moresby. Are there any other victims buried in your cemetery?"

"No, none that were infected."

"After we complete our examination they will be cremated. Their ashes will be returned to Keystone or disposed per your request."

"That's reasonable. No problem. We do our best to provide a peaceful resting place for our people."

"Our second objective is to destroy the mother, the matriarch, the spore body encapsulated in the iron meteor you accidentally penetrated with your diamond drill bit. For this we will use an aluminum-iron thermite bomb. At twenty-five hundred degrees Celsius, we expect to burn the fucking bitch to a crisp." Hemmingway stole a moment to let her expletive fuel Dawson's perception of her invincibility.

"Our third task is to plug the hole you drilled with the appropriate chemical fungicide cement. And lastly," she smiled wryly, "quarantine everyone in this area until all infected carriers are identified and… nullified."

"What the hell do you mean… nullified? We're talking about human beings, not some termites." Dawson remained unflappable, despite her subtle allegations of his complicity.

"Okay, let's call it euthanasia, if that is easier on your mind. Nevertheless, it has the same meaning. It is their choice. Anyone infected with viable spores will die a horrible death. If and when we find them, and they're still breathing, they'll be comfortably housed in isolation. Believe me, in the end, they'll be begging us to kill them. And it is my responsibility to make sure they do not experience that pain. Morphine is the solution to their suffering. But it is their choice."

Dawson interrupted. "May I ask how you test for viable spores in the human body?"

"Good question. It is actually very simple and painless. We use a bronchoscope, infrared thermal imager and pure oxygen. Doctor Jenkins will give you a personal demonstration."

Dawson immediately regretted asking.

The doctor opened his leather case and retrieved a thermal imaging bronchoscope and a small green flask of pure oxygen. He walked behind Dawson and gently, but firmly, cupped his hands around his ears. Dawson broke a nervous sweat.

"Now, lean back as far as possible. I will insert this bronchoscope down your throat, through your windpipe and into your lungs. I'll dispense a small quantity of pure oxygen into your lungs. If there are any viable spores they will fluoresce, and I will see them through the viewing optics."

Dawson understood what that meant. His leg began to shimmy, while he imagined the deadly game of Russian Roulette.

"Just relax. This won't hurt. You may get the urge to cough, but it will not last more than a few seconds. Here we go, nice and slow. Open your mouth – wider – wider – that's it – very good. Now take a deep breath – hold it – hold it – hold it. Good. Very good. He's clean." said Doctor Phillips, retracting the bronchoscope.

"Good for you, Mr. Elliott. Now about my security and recovery teams standing out there. There's thirty, plus us makes thirty-three. I understand you have a guest hotel."

"We do. It's a modest complex with a restaurant and maid service. There's plenty of rooms for you and your teams."

"Excellent. This entire area is now under quarantine. Nobody leaves without my personal approval. Armed guards are already in place. They will enforce the quarantine with orders to shoot. Anyone breaking the quarantine will spend thirty days in quarantine lockdown. I'll leave it up to you to advise your staff. Capisce?"

"Yeah, I understand." Dawson realized he was no longer in charge of his company.

"I want to make it perfectly clear that this is not a game, nor a training exercise. This is the real deal, potentially a global pandemic the likes of which we have never encountered in the history of mankind. There is no vaccine or cure on the horizon. With that, I would like Doctor McDermott to give you some background."

Doctor McDermott stood to make her presentation. "Thanks, Rachel. You might be wondering why someone from NASA would be a member of this team. It might surprise you to know that Lucifer, the name we gave to these fungi, was discovered by one of our Mars rovers several years ago. It too, was encased in an iron meteor, at least that was our best assumption. The rover's onboard analysis was limited. At first it appeared benign, until we exposed it to water. Within a few hours, Lucifer had sprouted several white stalks with red caps and white dots around the circumference. Additionally, slender roots, called mycelia, had grown from the base of each mushroom. Mycelia seek out nutrients. And when they locate a source of food, thread-like filaments called hyphae excrete enzymes which digest the nutrients. The data also suggests Lucifer reproduces asexually. When they flower, they eject thousands of sub-micron spores eager to populate a new host. All it takes is for someone to inhale one spore, one microscopic parasitic spore. Symptoms usually appear within twenty-four hours. Death occurs within the next twenty-four to forty-eight hours."

"How did you determine Lucifer was fatal to humans?" asked Dawson.

Quinn looked at Rachel for guidance.

"Go ahead. It's going to be on the Internet soon," said Rachel.

"Three years ago, NASA launched a manned mission to Mars. The astronauts' primary objective was to retrieve the Lucifer sample from the rover. Even though they were fully protected in EVA suits, they somehow became infected. Maybe they took off their helmets or had a leak in their suit. Both astronauts died on Mars, a man and a woman. They documented their own deaths on video. We've all seen it, up to the agonizing end. It's very graphic – Lucifer mushrooms everywhere – so terrifying, yet heartbreaking." Quinn choked and quickly wiped her eyes with the back of her hand.

Rachel broke the grim silence. "Let's take a break. I'm ready for that cup of coffee."

Everyone stood, took a deep breath and stretched their arms. Dawson suddenly thought he might have something that would spice up the conversation and perhaps shine a little light on some good news. He approached Rachel while she sipped her coffee.

"Hope it's strong enough for you. You know, there is something you didn't ask that is probably more important than the number of corpses."

Rachel gave him a patronizing glance. "And what might that be?" she said, taking a short sip of her coffee.

"We have a survivor!"

Rachel spilled her coffee. "What?" she bellowed. "Why the fuck didn't you tell me sooner?"

"You never asked. And you had the floor. I didn't want to interrupt your presentation."

Realizing this was probably the most important piece of information, she begged, "Where? Who?"

"He's here, in our ICU. He's not fully recovered, but our medical staff is confident he will be okay. His name is Tony Esperanza. His nickname is Snake – a worthy pseudonym for a man who survived the bite of three of the most poisonous snakes on the planet... *and the fucking Lucifer bitch..*"

"That's impossible." Rachel shook her head.

"Tony supervised the Gemini Falls core drilling operation. He watched his men die. We can walk to the medical clinic and pay him a visit. If he's awake, we'll have a little chat."

"Lead the way, Dawson. If what you said is true, it could be our first break in resolving this pandemic."

Dawson led the guests across the street to the medical center while contemplating how things had changed over the past few days. At first, he didn't appreciate Rachel's authoritarian approach. The arrival of outside professionals cast doubt on his leadership and raised the possibility that he was no longer calling the shots with respect to Keystone operations. On the other hand, perhaps Rachel and her band of CDC professionals would find a scientific resolution to the Lucifer outbreak and things might return to normal.

The modern, three-story medical center was home to a small contingent of doctors, physician assistants, registered nurses, LVNs, and Papuan support staff. Except for Doctor Kennedy, the medical team was entirely Papuans who had been trained at one of the two PNG medical schools. It was a modest operation, with limited surgical, radiological, pathological, and ICU capabilities. In addition to the reception area, the first floor included a conference center, cafeteria, waiting room, six examination rooms, and four ICU rooms. Forty double-bed rooms and two nurse stations filled the second floor. The upper deck contained private offices for the doctors, a dental clinic, segregated living quarters for shift workers, a small recreation room, and a laundry room. To the rear of the building, across a narrow concrete roadway, was a morgue capable of holding twelve bodies.

Most Keystone accidents involved men working in the open-pit or in the gold processing facilities. Minor injuries, including cuts, broken bones, and sprains were the most common. For those employed in the gold processing facilities, dust and toxic vapors triggered respiratory distress and caused chemical burns. Most medical emergencies were senseless accidents due to failure to follow proper safety regulations. For the most part, unlike the rainforest tribes, Keystone was a peaceful, law-abiding community with little discord or tribal infighting.

"Hello, Patricia. These are my guests. Is Tony awake? How's he progressing?" asked Dawson.

"He's been off the respirator since last night but he's still on oxygen. He even got up to *pis-pis* without any assistance. You can visit if you wish, but everyone will need to wear a disposable gown, mask, rubber gloves, booties, and head cap. The instructions are posted on the wall."

Patricia led the contingent down the hall to the ICU dressing room. "When you're finished, just toss everything in the proper bin."

After dressing in the appropriate attire, Dawson knocked softly on Tony's half-open door.

"Come on in." There was a lively spark in Tony's voice. "Dawson, good to see you. Look, no more respirator. Fuck am I glad to have that tube out of my throat. I felt like I was choking to death, but I guess I had no choice. They've got me hooked up to this oxygen, but said it was only for a few more days. I see you brought some visitors. Are we having a party or what? Who are these beautiful people?"

"All doctors – very astute doctors. This is Rachel Hemmingway. She's with the CDC – Head of Mycotic Investigations."

Rachel smiled. "Nice to meet you, Tony. Is it true you survived three poisonous snakebites?"

"Yup, cross my heart. It isn't something to brag about, but it has almost immortalized me."

Hemmingway introduced the other members of her team. "This is Doctor Quinn McDermott. She's with NASA – Principal Investigator for the Invasive Species Group."

Quinn smiled. "My pleasure."

"NASA? That's very interesting. I bet you know all about UFOs and space aliens."

"That information… well, much of it is classified. If I told you…"

Tony interrupted. "I know. You'd have to kill me," Tony chuckled.

"And this gentleman is Doctor Phillip Jenkins. He's Chief Scientist Pandemic Division – been with CDC for over twenty years."

"Hello, Mr. Esperanza. I'd like to shake your hand, but may I first conduct a painless test. I'd like to see what's inside your lungs."

Dawson interrupted, "I've already been tested. He's gonna see if there are any critters in your lungs. It's short and painless."

"Sure, go ahead. Do what you gotta do."

Jenkins retrieved his bronchoscope and thermal imagers. "Just lie back on your pillow. Open your mouth. I'm going to insert this down your windpipe and into your lungs. You're already breathing pure oxygen. That's good.

"Your lungs are clear. I did see some evidence of irritation, very similar to those I've seen from cat dander or pollen. But there is no sign of the Lucifer fungus."

"Hey, if I can kick ass on a death adder, fungus don't stand a chance."

"We need your help, Tony. You're the only human we know to have survived this Lucifer fungus. Would you be willing to help us find a cure or develop a vaccine? Billions of lives are at risk. You've seen what it can do to your friends and co-workers. It is very contagious, and we have no way to stop it – not yet anyway. That's why we need your help. You may be the lone survivor."

Tony didn't hesitate. "Sure. As soon as my doc says it's okay."

CHAPTER SEVEN

Two black helicopters crossed over Gemini Falls and turned west, heading up the Lagaip river to the Keystone core drilling site. Rachel, Dawson, and eight armed members of the recovery team were in the lead chopper. Quinn, Phillip, and eight armed personnel followed in the second chopper.

Everyone was dressed out in hazmat suits, otherwise known as MOPP, level-four, military grade personal protection equipment (PPE). This equipment provided the highest possible level of human protection against biological pathogens.

The one-piece, airtight disposable coveralls included a respirator, a neoprene rubber full-face mask with a panoramic clear plastic lens, and a UHF communication system. Unfortunately, the interior of the suit quickly became more like a sauna, which greatly limited the amount of time a human could effectively work in the heat and humidity of PNG. Footwear consisted of high-top rubber boots – the kind Alaskan crabbers wear in the open ocean.

"Gear up and tape up, people," ordered Rachel. "Check your respirators, seals, cuffs and double gloves. No gaps. No leaks."

Both helicopters circled the drill site at an altitude of two hundred feet.

Rachel was the first to see the carnage and her reaction was electrifying.

Rachel emitted an alarming scream. "Crocodiles! They're everywhere. The bastards are eating the corpses!"

"Jesus! This is insane," Dawson shouted. "My God, they're ripping my men to pieces… legs and arms, and… oh, no… heads too. They're fighting each other over body parts." Dawson bellowed. "Shoot the motherfuckers. Rachel, tell your men to kill them all."

The helicopters hovered while the CDC teams commenced to dispatch the ravenous beasts. Crocodile heads began to split apart. Their blood and tissue exploded in every direction. Even as they were being decimated with high-power rifles, the crocodiles continued their attack on the human corpses, mindlessly slashing their massive tails and snapping their jaws as bullet after bullet raced through their bodies.

Rachel grabbed a semi-automatic rifle and took aim on one of the bigger dragons. "Bingo, another one bites the dust." Taking aim again, she repeatedly pulled the trigger while hollering, "And another one bites the dust – and another – and another. Here, Dawson," exclaimed Rachel, handing him the weapon. "Take your best shot."

"No thanks. I think you've exterminated all of them. Let's get on the ground and take care of this messy business."

"What? My ears are ringing. I can't hear you."

Dawson read her lips and shouted, "Let's get on the ground."

Both helicopters landed seconds apart. Rachel was the first to exit. Dawson was next, followed by the first recovery team. Phillip, Quinn, and the second team gathered nearby. A few more shots were fired, mostly out of spite, but the battle was over.

Dawson shuddered at the sight. He recalled documentary films of Nazi extermination camps he had seen in his younger days. Only this was worse and much more haunting. His head filled with grisly images of his men – the merciless crocodile feeding frenzy – their eviscerated stomachs – limbs ripped from their sockets. It was more brutal than a wartime documentary – grislier than an ISIS beheading – a scene he'd never forget. Moments later he realized there was something missing.

"The tent!" he shouted. "The tent is gone. Someone stole the friggin tent."

Stunned by his assertion, Rachel cried out. "You're sure?"

"Absolutely. Teddy didn't bring anything back when he recovered Tony. The tent was here when they left. It was probably taken by natives." Dawson rushed to where the tent had been. "Look, Rachel. I almost stepped on them – Lucifer mushrooms. They're growing from under the wood pallets." Dawson gingerly stepped away.

""Rachel, come look at this," Quinn shouted. "There's more Lucifer mushrooms over here! They're everywhere – growing out of each corpse. My God, the mushrooms are sprouting from their mouths and noses." Nauseated, Quinn quickly covered her mouth and backed away while struggling to avoid vomiting.

"Goddamnit! How the hell are we supposed to deal with this? It's spreading faster than we can think."

Dawson realized Rachel had lost some of her bravado. She was no longer that cold-hearted, CDC superstar – the knight in shining armor. She had feelings and was as vulnerable and sensitive as most human beings. He also began to understand the enormity of the situation.

Devastated by the carnage, Rachel returned to her helicopter, sat on the open doorway, and began to sob. After a few deep breaths, she lifted her head, turned to her recovery team and spat out her commands.

"It's too damn bloody and dangerous to recover the remains. Burn everything! Burn the body parts! Burn the Goddamn crocodiles! Burn the whole fucking campsite!"

CHAPTER EIGHT

It was a time to trade, a flea market in the rainforest of sorts, a festive occasion for everyone, the young and old, men, women, children, and an occasional guest or tourist. It was also a celebration of life, marriage, and birth. Villagers from several nearby settlements had paddled, some for many hours, to join the *joewo* – a celebration of the pig.

They gathered along the riverbank adjoining the village. Some of the men were dressed in their ceremonial colors – faces painted in reds, whites and yellows, crowns of colorful songbird feathers and grass skirts. Each displayed an array of personal trophies, a cassowary claw through the nose, a necklace configured with wild pig tusks and crocodile teeth. While a quartet of sago drummers maintained the festive momentum, children danced and laughed. People came to trade their handicrafts, fruits, and decorated sago cakes, or meet old friends, share a story, or recount tales from the past.

The first to arrive were two Australian craft traders eager to purchase hand-crafted jewelry, spirit mask carvings, feathered headgear and other trinkets that they could sell to foreign tourists for outrageous profits. They were followed by scores of nearby villagers who had paddled many hours in handmade canoes. A young American man and his girlfriend arrived on a high-powered tour boat seeking a once-in-a-lifetime eco-adventure and the chance to mingle with indigenous highlanders – especially those with ancestors that were cannibals.

Pigs held a significant status in the everyday life of the highlanders and were the most treasured property of the Papuan natives. Pigs were often used to obtain a bride, pay off a debt, or resolve a dispute. Those who owned the most pigs were considered the upper class.

The task of slaughtering the pig was delegated to the men. While the women held the pig and fed the animal sweet potatoes as a distraction, the executioner dispatched the animal with an arrow to the heart. The women then gutted the carcass and washed the intestines of worms and parasites while the men placed the heart, lungs, and liver on bamboo stakes to dry in the sun. The animal was then baked with sweet potatoes in a pit filled with hot stones and covered with layers of palm and grasses. No one left the celebration hungry.

*****

Exhausted from the muggy weather and the clammy discomfort of her hazmat suit, Rachel had drawn a hot bath. She added a double measure of bubble bath suds and watched with anticipation as the warm water streamed from the spigot. She unsnapped her bra, stepped out of her panties, and gingerly lowered her sturdy frame into the effervescing water. As she let her buttocks, spine, and shoulders slide along the porcelain, the therapeutic solution rose past her ears and tickled her chin. She uttered a deep sigh and drifted to a more peaceful dimension.

Born in Boston to blue-blooded suburbanites, Rachel was an only child. She attended private schools through her teens and graduated from MIT with a PhD in microbiology. She once had a lover, an MIT post-graduate whom she left behind when she decided to accept a position at CDC headquarters in Atlanta. That was twenty years ago.

As expected, she'd traveled to many parts of the world, applying the most advanced microbiological techniques; risking her life to save the lives of others from deadly pathogenic organisms. She led the CDC efforts to contain an outbreak of SARS-D3, a mutated super-strain of the coronavirus that originated in China decades earlier. She championed the effort to curtail several recent outbreaks of Ebola. Her most legendary accomplishment was finding an effective treatment for candida auris, an insidious, drug-resistant fungus that had killed numerous healthcare workers and their patients throughout the globe.

The ringtone of her smartphone brought her back to reality. She sat upright, brushed the suds off her ear and retrieved her smartphone.

"Hello, Doctor Hemmingway?"

"Yes."

"It's David, David Stockton."

"David, nice to hear your voice. Are you in country?"

"I arrived in Port Moresby a few days ago. I would have called you sooner, but I was flat out getting settled. CDC asked me to set up a command and control center here. You and your team will now report through me. I think we can make your work more efficient. Do you have time to talk?"

"I'm soaking in the tub. Wish I could stay all day. But I'm glad they brought you into the theater. We need good leadership. What can we do to help?"

"We were all surprised to learn about the recent deaths of the Keystone drilling crew. The crocodile event was something new. It must have been a terrifying experience. You did the right thing."

"Bad news travels faster than good news."

"Well, things have definitely gotten worse. Yesterday, we received a call from the Wabag police. The story goes like this. One of the highland missionaries, Father Valencia, drove his ATV to a nearby village. Seems some of the regulars to his Sunday service didn't show up, so he rode his ATV down the muddy track to check on them. Well, as he approached the village, he found three corpses. He called the Wabag police and they dispatched a four-wheeler to investigate. What they discovered was way over the top. It appeared everyone in the village was dead – lying face down on the ground. Forty, maybe fifty natives – men, women, children. Many of the men were dressed in their celebration costumes. They had apparently cooked a pig – probably were having a party. Some pigs and chickens were wandering among the corpses."

"Goddamnit. Lucifer is getting way ahead of us – much faster than anything we've ever encountered. We've never experienced anything like this with any other fungus. But, you know, after the c. auris pandemic, I thought someday, something like this would happen. It's much worse than candidiasis. It's very contagious and has an incredibly short incubation period – two days max. What do you want me to do?"

"Get your team to the village asap. Clean it up as best you can. Recover what you need for research. I'll let you know if we want you to send anything to us. Let me know if you need any help. I'll text the GPS and my new contact information. Let me know what you find and be sure to get an accurate body count. Bring back a couple of corpses for tests in approved body bags. Burn the rest per CDC protocol."

"David, just so you know, we don't have any level-four facilities. I believe there's only space for twelve cadavers in the morgue. We have a few CDC body bags, but no sealable coffins. My team has limited PPE and I think we're gonna need a lot more before this bitch is contained. We can't handle more than a few infected bodies."

"I understand. We're working on a plan to establish a research and development effort here in Port Moresby. I expect to have a small team and level-four facility in the next couple of weeks. In the meantime, get your team mobilized to the village."

"We'll be airborne within the hour. Anything else?"

"We're working with the PNG government. They have made it very clear. They can't deal with this outbreak. It's way beyond their capabilities. They don't have the facilities, knowledge or infrastructure. We're going to take the lead. That's all I know right now. We'll talk later. Good luck. Stay clean."

"Hey, before you go, let me give you some good news. We have a survivor. He's been clean for over a week. Do you want me to send him to Port Moresby?"

"No. Keep him with you. There are some strategic decisions coming soon. I'll keep you posted. Oh, and one more thing. We picked up Father Valencia. He's in quarantine."

*****

It was ten-thirty in the morning when Jake Bronson and his trekking buddy, Scotty Ingram, stumbled from their taxi into the Port Moresby International Terminal. Still feeling the intoxicating effects of their last night of partying, they hauled their overstuffed backpacks through the terminal, huffing and puffing past the customs and immigration kiosks and finally to their departure gate. Qantas flight forty-four to Sydney was scheduled to depart at noon. After claiming their boarding passes, they both found a vacant spot near the picture windows and crashed.

"Hey, you two," the gatekeeper shouted while shaking Jake's shoulder. "Wake up. Your flight is boarding."

The two groggy trekkers grabbed their backpacks and hustled down the gangway. After showing their boarding passes to the attractive blonde stewardess, they found their seats.

"Fuck, mate. How come I always get stuck in the middle," Scotty grumbled.

"Cause you drink too much. Shutup and set your smelly ass down. Fuck, don't you ever take a shower?"

Scotty lifted his left arm and sniffed. "Ahh. Sweet as a rosebud. I need a beer."

"I'll buy the first round. Just sit your fuckin ass down and stop complaining. Shit, mate, it's a four-hour flight."

"Excuse me, gentlemen. I have the window seat," said the businessman as he shoved his briefcase into the overhead bin. "Sorry," he said while waggling across two sets of boney knees and flopping down in his seat. "Oh, excuse me, young man, but could you grab one of those little pillows for me. I need to get some winks on the way home."

"Sure." Jake retrieved a pillow and tossed it to the man. He then reached for his backpack and retrieved one of his souvenirs. "Look what I bought. It's a war mask I got at that village on the river – the one with the big white tent. I'm gonna hang it above my bar." Jake pulled away the newspaper wrapping, exposing the hand-carved relic. He blew away the village dust and held it up. "This is what the men wear when they go headhunting. Fuckers kill and eat their enemies wearing these."

Scotty coughed and blinked his eyes. "Hey, watch what you're doin, mate. Blowing fucking crap in my eyes. It stings – and smells like pepper." Tears fell from Scotty's angry eyes as he launched a sneezing fit.

"Pretty awesome, eh?" Jake traced his fingers over the hand-polished hardwood carving. "Ya think Molly will let me wear it to bed – you know, mate, like a naked warrior about to eat his prey?"

Still coughing, Scotty stuttered. "Not… if you were hoping to… to get laid. No way mate…Scotty, you're one crazy motherfucker. Put that stupid thing away and shut the fuck up. I need some shuteye."

"Excuse me, gentlemen. We're about to take off. Please fasten your seatbelts. We'll be taking drink orders soon," said the pretty blonde stewardess.

"I hope you've got plenty of cold Aussie suds. It's gonna be a long flight home," said Jake.

As she walked toward the cockpit, Jake held his gaze at her saucy swing while jabbing his elbow into Scotty's ribs. "Nice arse on that sheila, eh?"

CHAPTER NINE

"Quinn, this is Rachel. We have another outbreak – possibly an entire village."

"Damn, this bug must be rocket propelled. Where and when?"

"I just learned of it from David Stockton last night. He's the Deputy Director of Mycotic Diseases. He's here in Port Moresby setting up a command and control operation. That means this outbreak is priority number uno. Get the teams ready. Damn, I hate getting back into that fucking PPE in this humidity. I probably shouldn't complain. Every one of us is in the same bucket of shit. I'll meet you at the helicopters in thirty minutes."

*****

Depending on the circumstances, there were several ways to dispose of infected bodies. Everyone involved in the transportation and handling operations wore CDC compliant level-four personal protection equipment. Two teams were assigned to complete the mission. The first team documented the scene, obtained an accurate body count, identified and photographed the victims. The second team cremated the bodies and sanitized the killing zone. These specialists had two cremation options. If the body count was less than a dozen, exothermic cremation blankets were the most efficient. Each victim would be dowsed with a flammable disinfectant, then draped with an exothermic cremation blanket. When ignited, the blanket incinerated the body at fifteen hundred degrees Fahrenheit. Alternatively, when there were more than a dozen bodies, the CDC cremation team used a mobile, propane-fired, cremation retort. It was more efficient for cremating greater numbers of biohazard victims and reduced the corpse to a few pounds of grey ash in a few minutes.

*****

Like the opening scene from a *National Geographic* drone video, the helicopters descended until they were a few meters above the rainforest canopy. The tops of the village thatched-roof structures soon came into view, quickly followed by a panoramic view of the carnage. Dozens of dead Papuan natives lay scattered around an elongated ceremonial ground. The charred carcass of a partially dismembered pig swung from a nearby tree – a delicacy from a recent village feast. More bodies, men, women, and children, were scattered among the bamboo and grass structures and along the bank of the river, reminiscent of the aftermath of the battle of Gettysburg. The victims were all face down, some fully prone, others bent over at the waist as if they were giving homage to a divine spirit. Like a surreal petting zoo, a few sacred pigs and clucking chickens ambled amongst the corpses, totally oblivious to the devastation.

Repulsed beyond control, Quinn choked on her breakfast – swallowing hard so as not to soil the inside of her hazmat suit. After pausing to mentally decompress the nauseating knot in her stomach, she cleared her throat and shouted, "I can't believe this. It's so barbaric."

"Hang in there, girl!" shouted Rachel. "This isn't the first time you've seen the killing fields, and it won't be your last. Remember those Ebola outbreaks two years ago? Goddamn flies and maggots. The stench really got to ya."

"Rachel, there's no room to land in the village," shouted Captain Nixon.

"You'll have to walk in from the mission."

"Roger that. Let's head back to the mission."

Both helicopters returned to the mission and settled on the boggy terrain about eight hundred meters from the village.

The recovery team offloaded a lightweight ATV and a small, two-wheel trailer loaded with their equipment. The cremation team launched their mobile cremation retort along with several tanks of propane.

After double-checking their equipment, both teams traveled along the muddy road toward the village. They soon approached the first corpse – a young, barefoot woman wearing a pink cotton dress.

"Poor thing. What a tragedy. I hope she didn't suffer," said Quinn. "Oh, shit! There's those fucking Lucifer mushrooms growing out of her mouth and nose – same as the others."

"Take photos of her face, scars and tats. Estimate her age and tag her. We'll take her with us on the way back."

Farther down the road, they stood over a teenage boy dressed only in shorts – his face buried in the mud.

"Doctor Jenkins. Let's bag and tag this young man and take him to Keystone with the woman? Maybe we'll learn something."

At ground level, the devastation inside the village was far more macabre than the aerial view from the helicopter. It took a few minutes for everyone to come to grips with the madness.

"Everyone, fan out. Take plenty of photos. Let me know if you find something – a clue – anything out of place or suspicious."

As the teams searched the village they video recorded the devastation, counted the number of victims, noted their gender and estimated their age.

Suddenly Rachel saw something that triggered a recent memory. "Holy shit. It's the tent – the Keystone tent that Dawson said was missing from the Gemini Falls drill site."

Curious as a cat, she stepped through the opening. The interior was covered with woven grass mats. A collection of handicrafts, colorful feathered headgear, carvings, strings of kina shells, cassowary claws, wild boar tusks, and other souvenirs were proudly displayed.

"It's a native flea market," she yelled. "Quinn, you gotta see this."

As she walked through the tent, Rachel picked up a business card with the name and contact information of a Port Moresby craft trader. She rushed from the tent and shouted, "Has anyone found the body of a Caucasian man – probably Australian? Anyone?" There was no forthcoming affirmation from her team.

*****

Dripping with perspiration, Dawson was halfway into his morning workout when his smartphone rang. It was Benjamin Chambers, Vice Chairman of Keystone Resources.

"Good morning, Ben. How are you?" he said, wiping the sweat from his face.

"Not very well. In fact, I'm quite upset. What the hell is going on down there with all this CDC bullshit?"

This wasn't the first time Chambers had called in a panicked mood. He was from the old school where senior executives could vent their frustrations with intimidation and thundering outbursts. Dawson was quick to respond to the elderly Australian.

"I'm preparing a report for you and the board. Everything has happened so fast. It has nothing to do with mine safety. There's been a biological outbreak. A deadly fungus was discovered at the Gemini

Falls core drilling site. It was a *one-in-a-googol* accident – that's one followed by a hundred zeros. The team accidentally drilled into an iron meteor. It's crazy. Nothing like this has ever occurred before. CDC scientists say it's from outer space. We had no way of knowing it was there, that's for certain. I know it's hard to comprehend. Six of my men died at the drill site. We recovered one of the bodies but asked the Wabag medical examiner to recover the others. They called in the CDC. It was too dangerous for us – for anyone, really. The CDC calls it a level-four biological hazard."

"Stop right there. We know all about the CDC operations. We know they sent helicopters and agents to Keystone. We know they cremated the bodies at the drill site. We know Teddy and three of your medical staff have died from this mysterious outbreak. We know there is one survivor. It's all very messy."

"All that, and more, will be in my report. CDC just returned from another outbreak at one of the highland villages. I'll have more data after speaking with them."

"I didn't know about that. Goddamnit, Dawson. I know it's not your fault. There will be lawsuits. Our exposure may be greater than our assets. I'm afraid it could bankrupt the company. Listen, Dawson, we've just received a letter from the PNG Prime Minister, co-signed by the Minister of Interior and Minister of Health. The government has nationalized our mine."

Depending on your resilience and fortitude, it was the kind of news that could drive a spike in your heart. *"Nationalized Keystone? Can they do that?"*

"They sure as hell can. We don't own it. We lease the property from the government. They have the right to terminate the agreement at any time."

"What about all the equipment – the employees?"

"The rolling stock, process equipment, and supplies belong to us. Do you have any idea what it's worth… fucking pennies on the dollar? Scrap! That's all. Scrap. Those new million-dollar loaders we just bought are virtually worthless. Maybe when this is over, the Chinese will buy them – turn them into razor blades. I don't know what we'll do with the aircraft. Everything is leased."

"And the process facilities, offices, apartments, hotel."

"All leasehold improvements belong to the government. That's the agreement. But they don't want to take over the mine – not now – maybe never."

"But I have two thousand employees and a staff of professionals, engineers, logistics, medical people."

"You and your salaried staff will receive termination letters. It will include a week's pay for every year of service, plus accrued vacation. All hourly employees will receive two weeks' severance plus vacation time. The HR department will handle the details. I had to take the Chairman to the mat on this. He wanted to close it down with nothing more than a thank-you letter."

"Thanks for your generosity. So, that's it. We're done."

"I'm afraid so. You can be proud of your accomplishments. The company enjoyed record profits under your leadership. I'm sorry it had to end this way."

"No more than I. You know, we found another ore deposit, perhaps more promising than Keystone. Maybe this Lucifer outbreak will be short-lived. Maybe it will be contained. Science has always found a cure or vaccine for the flu, malaria, coronavirus. Are you prepared to walk away with nothing but heartbreak?" Dawson knew the answer before he asked the question.

"Good luck, Dawson."

*****

Dawson shuffled to his liquor cabinet, poured himself a double scotch and slumped into his easy chair. After taking a long swallow, he allowed the tepid liquid to trickle down his throat, then closed his eyes. Feeling empty, he tried to envision his future, but all he saw was the past. It had been an exciting ride – more invigorating and memorable than he had expected when he first began his career.

For three years, his first wife, Karen, bore the brunt of his swashbuckling lifestyle. He remembered the day – a Friday afternoon. He'd been gone for two months. As he opened the front door, he called out her name. Her note was on the floor. She was thankful they had not shared a child, but it was time for her to move on.

Cece immediately came to mind. Maybe they could work it out. He believed he loved her or was it something less. Maybe she was right. Maybe it was all about the sex and not much else. The idea of being a couple felt warm and gratifying. But the notion she might want him to settle down – to give up his globetrotting escapades, or perhaps start a family, put a knot in his stomach. On the other hand, maybe she wanted to live the rest of her life as he had – scattering her seeds to the wind.

He was too old and set in his ways to be a father. He didn't know where or when he would find another job. And then there was Lucifer – this grotesque killer. What if the CDC failed to contain it? What if the entire world was in peril? What if…?

He swallowed the rest of his drink and dialed her number.

"Hi, Dawson," she answered, huffing. "I just finished a workout and a hot shower. It's good to hear your voice. How's everything at the mine?"

"I have some bad news. I got fired today," he blurted.

"What? Fired? What's going on?"

"The government nationalized the mine. There was a biological outbreak at the Gemini Falls site – a deadly fungus. It has killed several of our people and many native villagers. The CDC has a posse of scientific investigators here trying to find a way to stop it, but from what I understand, they are not having much luck. I've lost some good friends and employees. It's hard for me to talk about it. So sad. Enough about me. Are you still in Port Moresby?"

"Yes. As a matter of fact, I got the contract to explore for rare earth deposits in one of the most remote areas of PNG. I'm excited to be working, but don't fancy being so far away from civilization. I'm leaving in a few days heading up the Sepik to some godforsaken, croc-infested outpost called Pagwi."

"Pagwi? That's way out in the boonies. I'm familiar with that area. The Sepik is magical. For thousands of years, ever since humans first came to PNG, the Sepik has been the river of life for natives. It's a sacred, living body filled with mystery and myths. You'll either love it or despise it. I love the Sepik. It's the longest river in PNG – seven hundred miles. There is some interesting geology up the Karawari and Yuat tributaries. But that's another two or three days upriver from Pagwi, through some very hostile areas. I've often thought the highland geology might be ideal for rare earths. It's rough terrain with lots of poisonous snakes and other nasty creatures. I hope you're not working alone."

"It's me and two geology post-grads from the university. We plan to stay in the villages, in grass huts on woven mattresses under mosquito nets. I know what life is like in the outback. The highlands of Vietnam are very similar. And I don't mind showering under a rain-filled bucket, or crapping in the bush. Don't worry about me, I can take care of myself."

"That's for sure. Nobody knows that better than me. You're as tough as they come, Cece. I've never doubted that. I'm delighted you got a contract, and I don't doubt you can handle the outback. But there's some crazy shit going on around here –a biological hazard – people are dying horrific deaths. The CDC gave it a name – Lucifer. We've lost six men at the Gemini Falls core drilling site. That's the place the Smaark kid showed us. The CDC has set up their operations in Keystone."

"I'm sorry about your losses, but – nationalizing Keystone. Fuck, that's atrocious. Maybe they know something you don't. Maybe this so-called biohazard is a much more serious problem."

"I'm worried you might get exposed. It's not pretty."

"I know you care. I really do. And I'm sorry you lost your men and your job. What are you going to do?"

Her question opened the door to his imagination. "I have a home in Bali. It's on Kuta beach, one of the most beautiful beaches in the world. There's lots of palms, flowers, friendly people, great shopping, excellent bistros and awesome scenery. The water is warm and clear – perfect for sailing and diving. You'd love it. We'd have a great time together."

"You'll be bored to death in Bali. I know you inside and out. You need to stay busy. Take some time off, enjoy the beach nymphs, get laid – every night. But like I said, I know you. Two – maybe three months and your skin will be crawling with boredom. Dawson, my love, when the time comes to end your journey in Shangri-La, you'll take whatever adventure they offer because you need that more than you need me."

Her response closed the door to his imagined utopia. "Maybe we could just take a long trip together? See the sights of Europe, Alaska, wherever. Wouldn't you like to join me? You know how much I care – I love you, Cece, and I want you by my side. We'll have a great time."

"That's one hell of an offer, but you sound like you're desperate. We've had some great times and wonderful nights. I've always enjoyed being with you very much. But I have plans and aspirations too. I can't go running off to Bali or any other place – at least for the foreseeable future."

Her words were like thorns – the more she spoke the truth, the deeper they dug into his heart. He knew what she said was true. He had felt it himself, many times. When it comes to love and marriage, adrenaline junkies have a terrible track record. Finding a balance between the one you love and the call of the wild is a vintage struggle. Torn between two lovers, she chose what she believed to be in her best interests.

"You need to find another project. Go back to Nevada. Three of the biggest gold mines in the world are there – Carlin-Neva, Goldstock, and El Cortez. It's all desert –one big beach party. That's what you need. That's what drives you and keeps you sane. There's lots of sunshine and cold beer to ease your mind in the desert. Let them do their magic."

"You're breaking my heart, girl." Under humbling duress, Dawson abruptly ended the call. "Hey, good luck. Be careful. Call if you change your mind."

"Goodbye, Dawson."

"Goodbye, Cece."

*****

Rachel knocked on Dawson's apartment door. It was late in the afternoon and he'd just finished boxing up some of his books and labeling them *Bali* with a felt-tip pen.

"Come on in. The door is unlocked," he shouted, somewhat irritated at being disturbed while cogitating where to put his rubber boots.

"Hello, Dawson. What's with all the boxes? Are you leaving?"

Dawson cast a distressed glance and continued with his task.

"I'm getting the fuck outta PNG. They don't want me anymore and the feeling is mutual. Bali here I come," he replied while continuing his search for a suitable place for his boots.

"Let's talk. Come, sit down and listen to what I have to say."

Flustered by the interruption, Dawson dropped his boots on the hardwood floor and mumbled, "Okay, okay. But I need a drink first. Can I get you anything?"

"Sure, white wine if you have it. Otherwise scotch on the rocks."

"Today is not a wine day – not enough liquid courage." Dawson poured two fingers of scotch in two crystal glasses. "Let's sit on the porch. This place is too depressing."

After settling into lounge chairs, Dawson crossed his legs and lifted his glass. "Bottoms up." Their glasses touched with a sharp ting.

"I know who called you today. And I know why," confessed Rachel. "Sorry about that. I can see you're in the process of moving. What are your plans?" A sliver of a grin appeared in the corners of her mouth.

Dawson raised a brow. "Can you tell me what the fuck is happening? Where are you going with this biological warfare shit?"

"We've got to get Lucifer under control. Our computer models… well, you don't want to know. I've been talking with one of my bosses, David Stockton. He's the Deputy Director of Mycotic Diseases at CDC. Well, we, I mean the top dogs at CDC briefed the Prime Minister and senior members of the PNG parliament. Since the epicenter of this fungus appears to be in the highlands of Enga province, the most logical place to set up a level-four operation is the Keystone mine. It is the least populated area with the space and facilities for centralizing our operations. That is why the Papuan government nationalized the mine."

"I'm not surprised," he snapped, shaking his head.

"They asked us, the CDC, to take charge of combating this biological hazard. They will support us with provincial medical services, police, and security forces as best they can. Frankly I don't think they will be able to deal with the medical or social consequences. This parasitic fungus has already killed many people and we expect many more victims before we get any sort of stopgap measures in place. We don't know much about Lucifer, but we need to be close to the epicenter and require a suitable facility to conduct our research. Now that Tony Esperanza has fully recovered, we hope he will be able to help us get a handle on it. However, as of now, we haven't learned much from his test results."

"Why is this happening here in PNG and not someplace like Siberia?"

"From our NASA experience, we know for a fact it did not originate on earth. Therefore, it came here from another part of the universe. As to why it's in PNG and not Siberia – we don't know that it is not in Siberia – buried for eons under hundreds or even thousands of feet of ice, mud, permafrost, lava, sedimentary deposits. It may be under LA, or Singapore or Paris. Your discovery was purely accidental. Here on earth, there are a hundred thousand species of fungi – about ten thousand of them are parasitic fungi species that invade and eventually kill their hosts. Some of them invade and kill humans."

"Oh, fuck. That's what scares me the most." Grimacing, Dawson squirmed in his chair and scratched his head.

"All we know for sure is that it attacks the lungs. Interestingly, that is the most common source of infection in humans by other fungal species here on earth. When the mushroom flowers, thousands of microscopic spores are ejected into the air. If inhaled, it only takes one, just one sub-micron spore to infect and eventually kill a human. Once Lucifer spores are inhaled, they grow inside the lungs. From our autopsies, we know the root system, the mycelium and hyphae, attach to the alveoli, depriving the victim of oxygen. The victim suffocates."

"But why do the victims appear to commit suicide, face down on the ground?"

"While most victims are found face down, some are curled in a fetal position and others are lying on their backs. Like many earthly fungi, there may also be a psychotropic element that drives victims to die on or near the ground. This may trigger or facilitate the growth of the mycelium and allow them to extend their roots into the soil. Once the victim dies, the mushrooms emerge seeking another source of nutrients."

"Why only humans? Why not other animals, birds, snakes, any air breathing creature?" asked Dawson.

Rachel teased a sip from her glass of scotch, pursed her lips and shook her head. "We have no fucking idea. So far, we have about sixty human victims, men, women and children. We haven't seen any dead animals. That doesn't mean that they are not infected, we just haven't seen them. Maybe they wander off and drown like some crickets and grasshoppers do when infected by Cordyceps. Or maybe they are driven to hide in a tree or inside a hole. Until we find evidence animals are at risk, we'll assume their spores only infect humans."

Dawson's face blanched – a crest of nausea swelled in his stomach. He quickly took a long swallow of scotch to squelch the revulsion, then swallowed the last gulp and reached for the half-empty bottle.

Dawson lost his train of thought. "Excuse me, Rachel. Give me a moment to... how long will it take to get control of this fungus among us... excuse my trope?" Dawson forced a giggle while refilling his glass.

"Fungus among us. That's cute. Listen, the fact is I have no idea. It might be a year – it might be never. I know it's hard to get your head around this, but to be brutally honest, many millions, possibly billions... could perish."

"In other words, the world as we know it might end."

Rachel closed her eyes, rubbed her forehead and nodded positively. "Will you pour me another drink – a double."

Dawson filled both glasses and began to envision the rest of his life. It was filled with clouds and fuzzy visions.

Rachel reclaimed her focus. "I'd like to make you a job offer. The Keystone mine is as close to the epicenter of this disaster as we should be. Everything we need to set up a quick response and research center is right here. The PNG government owns it and wants us to use it. There's room to extend the runway for larger aircraft. We're gonna see a lot of air traffic, from heavy-lift choppers to jumbo jets. There are comfortable accommodations for many more people too. There's a hospital and space to add research labs. You've got heavy equipment needed to move dirt and build the runway. In other words, Keystone is the perfect location. Now, all we need is someone to be the prime mover – an experienced manager to run this operation.

CDC has mobilized a few mycotic experts who will be based here. We're gonna need a place for them to live and work, places to shop, eat, and relax. We'll need machinery repair shops, helicopter hangars, trucks, and more mobile crematoriums. None of this will happen if we don't have someone in charge. It's a logistics nightmare, and I can't think of anyone better qualified for the job than you. How about it, Dawson? The salary plus hazard pay is competitive and you can keep your office and whatever staff you need."

Dawson took another sip of his drink and exhaled a heavy breath. "Whew! I'm overwhelmed. I appreciate your confidence. But before I decide I'd like to get a better idea of what we're dealing with and what this place would look like if you had everything you needed to prevent Lucifer from destroying humanity."

"Glad you asked. I'm probably the best person to ask. It is my specialty. But you already know that. So, sit back and let me give you the condensed edition of the fungi kingdom."

"I'm all ears." Slightly numbed by the liquor, he leaned back and tried to clear the cobwebs from his head.

"There's over a million different species of fungi on earth. Most scientists believe they originally came to earth in a panspermia event – aboard a comet or meteor – maybe billions of years ago. The biggest mushroom lives in the Blue Mountains of Oregon. It's at least eight thousand years old. The body is underground and is about three miles in diameter."

"Three miles? Jesus, I hope it's not a maneater."

"It actually produces edible mushrooms. The Italians love them for spaghetti. But I digress. One family of parasitic fungi, Cordyceps, has over four hundred species that kill insects, animals, and plants. Their sole purpose is self-propagation. An example is the *Ophiocordyceps unilatereralis*. It thrives in tropical forests and infects ants. Their spores penetrate the exoskeleton and gradually take over their behavior, compelling the ant to find a stem or leaf that is ideally suited for spore dispersal and optimizing the chance for infecting another host. The ant sinks its mandibles into the leaf or stem and dies. Later, the fruiting body, the mushroom, erupts from the ant's head and ejects several thousand spores into the atmosphere where the wind may carry them hundreds, perhaps even thousands of miles. Some spores rise thousands of feet into the atmosphere. They've found spores from Mexico in Canada.

"We see similar behavior in the victims here in PNG. They are beaconed by some physiological force to die in the boggy ground where the fruiting body, the red mushroom we find growing out of the victim's mouth and nose, can eject its spores. Remember, the primary goal of the mushroom is to find and infect another host."

"Jesus Christ. That's depressing as hell. Scares the crap out of me." Dawson shuddered while shaking his head. He'd seen what happened to Lenny and the drill crew. Images of their bodies whirled inside his head. He asked himself the big question. Did he really want to die like that?

"How come Tony survived?"

"We don't know. We're still conducting tests."

"So, everyone who wants to live must wear a level-four biohazard suit."

"Only if they're likely to be exposed to Lucifer spores. That's one of the major reasons CDC wanted to set up operations in Keystone. It's close enough to the epicenter, but far away from major population centers."

*****

Dawson couldn't sleep. The scotch didn't help. It just fractured the dreams into pieces of a bigger puzzle. One minute he was dreaming of sitting on Kuta Beach enjoying a beer and the sight of bikini-clad women frolicking in the surf. The next minute he was pondering a potentially life-threatening endeavor managing the Keystone CDC operation. He'd always been an explorer, a swashbuckling adventurer.

That was the reason he could never develop a long-term relationship. Most of the women in Dawson's life were either more reckless than he, or were hooked on a cosmopolitan environment – shopping malls, chatty friends, social functions, dinner parties, theater dates, a big, beautiful home with a pool, a sexy late-model coupe and some high-speed freeways leading to the nearest boutique, spa, or beauty salon. Toss in a couple of kids and, *"oh my gosh,"* you have an imaginary happy urban family.

No doubt, that was not Dawson's dream. So here he was, exactly where the Good Lord wanted him to be. If only Cece would join him, his life would be damn near perfect.

*****

"Hello, David. I was hoping it was you."

"Hi, Rachel. We found your missing Port Moresby craft dealer. You were right, he's Australian. One of his assistants found his body. He had the same symptoms as the others. Unfortunately, his assistant is now sick and confined in our quarantine area. We've also locked down his retail gift shop, but it's probably too late. Hundreds of international tourists have been exposed – Australians, Europeans, Americans, Japanese, etc. etc. You and I both know what that means."

"Oh, yeah. I certainly do. Goddamnit. What else is happening? Got any good news?"

"I wish I did. We just got word from CDC Sydney. They've recovered two victims, both males in their early twenties. A patrol officer found them on Bondi Beach. He did the right thing – called police headquarters, described the condition of the bodies and they contacted local CDC office. CDC sent a biohazard team to their apartment. They found a wooden mask carving from PNG. If I had to take a guess, I'd say these two blokes were at the village where you found the tent and the business card of the Port Moresby craft trader. CDC removed and burned all the furnishings and sanitized the apartment."

"I'm not surprised. We'll probably see more of these outbreaks all over the world."

"How's Quinn doing with her lab work? Any news on Tony, our lone survivor?"

"She's doing everything possible to sort it out. Blood tests, RBC, WBC, platelets, glucose, pH, occult blood, enzyme and protein analysis, potassium, dissolved gas, EKG, EEG, XYZ, you name it – she's either done it or plans to. I do have some good news. Dawson Elliott has decided to stay on and help us run the Keystone facility. I'll send you the paperwork. He's agreed to GS fifteen, level ten, plus hazard pay."

"Great. He'll be a big help. Let me know what you need. Good luck."

"Thanks for the call."

CHAPTER TEN

A battalion of Australian Army Corps of Engineers were the first to arrive in the port city of Lae together with an armada of heavy-duty construction equipment and an equal number of large flat-bed trucks to haul them from Lae to Keystone. Although Keystone had a fleet of giant ore carriers, dozers, backhoes, and scrapers, the Australians brought cement mixers, tamping machines, and pavers. Day and night, a caravan of trucks loaded with cement, steel rebar, and other building materials were shuttled from Lae to Keystone.

The roadway was frightfully dangerous – a three-hundred-mile odyssey on a narrow, rain-soaked roadway illogically named the Highland Highway. The two-lane blacktop weaved through the Markham Valley, crawled over the five-thousand-foot-high Kassam Pass into the Eastern Highlands. After crossing the Yonki Dam, it slogged through the towns of Kainantu and Henganofi to the provincial capital of Goroka. From Goroka, the road skidded over the eight-thousand-foot Daulo Pass, across the Simbu Province to Kundiawa – the start of the Western Highlands. It then zigzagged its way through the highland rainforest to Wabag, while being pummeled by falling rocks and dodging numerous potholes. After a fifteen-hour journey through purgatory, these road warriors finally reached the Keystone open-pit gold mine. Here, they immediately commenced their first project – to extend the existing runway and make it suitable for large cargo and passenger aircraft. Within a week, there was more heavy-duty earth-moving capacity in Keystone than anywhere else in the world.

*****

Dawson sat on his porch, a double scotch on the rocks in one hand, the other resting on his knee. The setting sun radiated an array of red, yellow, and orange plumes that shape-shifted to an equally beautiful panorama with each passing minute.

He could hear it coming – the enormous fracture radiating from deep inside the belly of the mother earth. Nothing to worry about. It was just another earthquake – a magnitude six – the same strength and duration observed several times a month along the Ring of Fire. As the ground began to shake and shimmy, the seismic waves sounded eerily like the thunderous rumblings of a jumbo-jet accelerating down the runway.

One violent tremble was followed by several smaller wiggles. Collectively, they produced just the right set of vibrations to cause the dust on his porch to levitate, as did the powdery residue across the terraced levels of the mine. A moment of introspection squeezed tiny beads of sweat from his brow. "Why the hell am I still here?" he mumbled.

Rachel and her team were deployed to another outbreak. As expected, it was a riverside highland village with approximately two hundred inhabitants. Knowing the virulence of Lucifer, they didn't expect to find any survivors. Two helicopters departed, twelve CDC agents in each one, plus a third helicopter equipped with two mobile crematoriums and a team of CDC operators..

The mobile crematorium was an efficient machine. A few minutes after the body was inserted in one end – three to five pounds of grey dust came out the other. The cycle time varied depending on body weight. A one-hundred-and-fifty-pound cadaver took five minutes. It was the quintessence of "dust-to-dust" dogma.

*****

The jingle of his smartphone brought him back to reality.

"Dawson, it's me. Tony."

"Tony! It's great to hear from you. How are you, man?"

"I'm damn near perfect. I've been cooped up in the level-four lab for over a month. No phone. No outside communication. I had to beg them to call you. I'm tired of the needles, probes, brain scans, and MRIs. What's going on at the mine?"

"What mine? There is no mine. They shut it down. PNG nationalized the whole damn thing. CDC turned it into an operations base for dealing with this fungal outbreak. You gotta see this place. It's crazy."

"Yeah, that's crazy all right. What are you doing there?"

"They offered me a job to run the joint. Mostly logistics. My job is almost the same as before – control of material, equipment, and personnel. We still have most of the ex-pat staff and native medical team, but the natives have left. They said this place was haunted by evil spirits. I probably should have gone to my home in Bali, but Cece didn't want to run away with me and they're paying me good money to stay. If you're free to leave, why don't you join me? I could sure use your help."

"I can't leave just yet. CDC owns me until they take my last drop of blood. But I really don't mind. Hey, if I can help find a cure or vaccine for this motherfucker, so be it."

"You know, Tony, they gave it a name – Lucifer."

"Yeah, I heard. Lucifer! How appropriate is that?"

"It's easy to remember. Are they making any progress with your tests?"

"Quinn, er, Doctor McDermott, has been up front with me about the purpose for each test and what they hope to discover. They found trace evidence of something like a protein, a chemical that may function as physiological or behavioral factor, but they have not been able to accurately define it. I'm as clean as a fresh diaper. I don't have any symptoms, been breathing normal, am not coughing or wheezing. Shit, man, I'm ready to rock-n-roll. My biggest problem is my, you know, libido. I think that's the correct word. Libido. Now I know what it's like to be in prison without any conjugal visits. What I really need is a nymphomaniac."

"Sorry, mate. I don't keep a little black book anymore."

"You know, Dawson, I was devastated to learn that Teddy, Doc Cato and his nurses succumbed from this Lucifer bug. I regret calling you for help. They might still be alive."

"Hey, don't beat yourself up about it. Shit happens. You thought you were going to die like Lenny and the others. It's not your fault they perished. Cato made a mistake. He didn't wear the proper protective gear. Neither did his nurses. Teddy was just doing his job. He wasn't close to the bodies, but I guess the spores somehow blew into his lungs and… well, we know what happens after that." Dawson choked on his words.

"I still feel responsible."

"Don't worry about it. You're doing everything possible to help find a cure. No one will ever doubt your integrity or courage. I hope to see you soon. Until then, you take care."

"You too, Dawson. We'll keep in touch. So long for now."

*****

Rachel opened the door to her apartment, staggered to her bedroom and flopped down onto her bed. She grasped a pillow, covered her face and began to sob.

She couldn't get the images of death out of her head. It was the fourth village she had incinerated – another two hundred and sixty men, women, and children, bringing the total death count on her watch to over a thousand.

The most heartbreaking and gut-wrenching reflections were of the babies – many of them cradled in their mother's arms. She had been unable to watch her team gather up their tiny corpses and place their limp bodies into the crematorium. She despised the sights and sounds of the flaming retort. It reminded her of the biblical prophecies of hell – the devils' doing – a remorseless inferno – punishment for evil sinners. She always felt a surge of nausea when she heard the hiss of the propane, for it fueled the inferno and turned all human flesh and bones into sterile grey dust regardless of gender, age, color, or creed. Unable to chase the nightmares from her head, she cried herself to sleep.

*****

It was five in the morning when Dawson awoke, driven by the compelling pressure in his bladder. He had endured a restless night. He had a headache and a sore throat and was experiencing a few sneezing and coughing spells. He stumbled to the latrine and shortly finished his business. Thirsty, he turned on the light and looked in the mirror. The reflection of his puffy eyes spooked him. Like an electrical shock, a flash of panic rushed into his imaginings. Suddenly weak and dizzy, he grasped the countertop, steadied himself and made a closer inspection of his face.

"No!" he shouted, squinting his bloodshot eyes. He coughed, then grabbed a tissue to clean his face. He felt a sneeze brewing and quickly captured it with his tissue. A trickle of blood dripped from his left nostril. "No! Goddamnit, no!" he shouted. "This can't be. I've never been near infected victims." He wiped away the blood and shook his head in denial. "Fucking hell. I should have gone to Bali. I was a fool to stay in this godforsaken hellhole. Stupid son of a bitch." He slapped his cheek with an open hand as he considered the possibility he might soon be dead.

Devastated by the deadly symptoms he had come to fear, he lumbered into his kitchen, poured himself a glass of cold water, and slumped into a chair. His thoughts quickly segued to Cece. She was out there in the rainforest, the same rainforest that spawned Lucifer. The love and longing for her rushed into his heart. "I should have been a better man. I should have considered her ambitions and understood her pleas. But I was selfish and overbearing. God, I really do love her," he whispered.

With his glass of water in hand, he rushed to the bedroom to retrieve his phone. With trembling fingers, he dialed Cece. Her phone rang... and rang... and rang. Thinking she was not available, Dawson was about to hang up when she answered.

"Hello," she whispered with a sleepy inflection.

"Cece. It's me, Dawson."

"It's five in the morning. Are you okay? You sound like you have a cold or flu."

Dawson held back a sneeze. "Sorry to wake you, but I need to tell you something important and I don't think I'll have another chance to say it. I think I've got the Lucifer infection." Dawson sneezed into his tissue, then gagged on his words. "I've got... some of the... symptoms."

"Oh, no," she wailed. "My God, Dawson, I'm speechless. I don't know what to say. This is terrible. I'm so sorry. Are you sure?" Cece held her tears but was angry at the world.

"No, I'm not sure. I've got to call Rachel. She'll undoubtedly place me in quarantine and order some tests. I might not have much time. This Lucifer bug... well... from what I know... it won't be more than another day to two. Listen, please. I want you to know how much I love you, and how much I have missed your sweet kisses and our lovemaking. Those were very special moments. I've been selfish, and

I've hurt you. I didn't mean to. I'm sorry I was so obsessed with my work. So sorry. I hope you can find it in your heart to forgive me."

Cece was mad, not at Dawson. She was mad at the world – mad at her maker.

"This isn't the way to go out, Dawson. You deserve better. We both deserve better. You know I care. And yes, it could be much more than that. I've been selfish too. Little Miss career builder. Yep, that's me, Cece the whiz-kid, the go-getter, the fearless explorer, soon to be famous discoverer of rare earth elements. I guess neither of us will reach our fountainhead. But enough about that. Now you listen to me, Dawson Elliott, and listen well. You can fight this thing. You can cast it out and kill it. I know you can achieve anything you put your mind to. I want to help you get through this, but I'm stuck in Wewak."

"I thought you were working in Pagwi, under contract to PNG."

"I was until they quarantined my area of exploration. They shut down all river traffic to and from Pagwi. I expect they'll cancel my contract too. They're not going to pay me to sit on my ass. You hang on, Dawson. If you don't beat this bug, I'll kick your ass."

"I love it when you talk dirty. But seriously, thanks, Cece. I appreciate your confidence. Now you listen to me. I love you with all my heart. I will always love you, even after I'm… oh, never mind. Where are you now?"

"Port Moresby. The Hyatt. Our favorite hotel. I'm desperate to see you, but there are no flights. The airport is on lockdown indefinitely. I'm afraid I'm marooned at the Hyatt."

"Stay put. I'll send the Sikorski. The Hyatt has a rooftop landing pad. Our pilot will call you just before he arrives. You won't be allowed to board the helicopter unless… you know… you're clean. I'll arrange for someone from the CDC to test you at the Hyatt."

*****

"Doctor Hemmingway, Rachel, this is Dawson. Sorry to bother you."

"Hello, Dawson. You're up early."

He wrestled with disclosing his presumptive diagnosis. "I... I might have it... Lucifer. Can someone come to my apartment and administer the test? I ache all over, puffy eyes, bloody nose, sneezing and coughing. I need to know if... you know what I mean."

It was the first time in his life that the thought of dying was much more than a whimsical passing. He'd seen others die, mostly from accidents around heavy equipment and mishandling of explosives. But Lucifer, Lucifer was final. There was no cure, and it was quick.

"Let's not get ahead of ourselves. Stay put. Give me a half-hour to dress out and grab my test equipment."

The ambulance arrived with flashing red lights and the sinusoidal shriek of an obnoxious siren. Dressed in white, level-four coveralls and carrying a respirator, Rachel and one of her EMTs rushed into Dawson's apartment.

He was sitting up in his bed, sipping a glass of scotch.

"Scotch? You said you were sick. Why am I not surprised?" snapped Rachel.

"It's liquid courage. I'm celebrating my less than awesome life and I'm not going down without a fight or a party."

"Your optimism is commendable, but I need to conduct a test. You've had this test before. May we proceed?"

"Okay," he replied, placing his glass on the table and leaning back.

Rachel scanned his forehead with an infrared thermometer. "Ninety-nine, point six. Low grade fever. Nothing to worry about. Now let's peek inside your lungs."

"Sure thing, Doc." Although he knew the test would reveal the truth, he tried to give Hemmingway the impression he was omnipotent by faking a wide smile.

"You know the drill. Open your mouth."

Rachel retrieved her thermal imaging bronchoscope and the bottle of pure oxygen.

"Now, lean back as far as possible while I insert my bronchoscope."

His muscles tensed and he gagged as she pushed the scope through his airway.

Dawson would know his fate in seconds. He was terrified. But with every ounce of willpower he tried not to show it.

She carefully inserted the bronchoscope into his throat, triggered a puff of oxygen and looked for any signs of Lucifer spores through the viewing optics.

Daunting visions danced through his mind and he broke into a cold sweat. With each passing second he felt his heartbeat thundering in his temples, counting down his destiny to a life or death verdict, the ultimate judgement from the Almighty.

As she scanned the interior of his lungs, Rachel remained stoic, offering neither a hint of yea nor nay. For Dawson, those few seconds were petrifying.

"There is no sign of Lucifer. You have the flu."

Dawson's eyes flew wide open. "Whew! That's the best news I've had in my entire life. Thanks, Rachel. I feel like I've been reborn."

"I'll give you some meds to relieve your congestion. You'll be back on your feet in a couple of days. Take care of yourself, Dawson. You're a valuable leader and we need you on our team. By the way, I sent one of my nurses to test your friend Cece before she boarded your helicopter. She's clean and is on her way here. I hope it all works out for you both."

Dawson was awestruck with her compassion – a characteristic she had seldom shared with him. "Thanks, Rachel. That means a lot to me. And thanks for the rapid response. I really thought I was going to die."

*****

Cece leaped out of the helicopter, grabbed her bags and rushed to the Keystone apartment complex. She took the elevator to the executive floor and knocked on Dawson's door. Not knowing what to say, or how to react, her heart skipped a couple of beats while a lump formed in her throat.

"Come on in," he shouted from his bedroom.

Upon entering, she dropped her bags in the hall and hurried into the living room. Dawson was sitting up, holding a glass of scotch on one hand, while the fingers of his other hand pinched assorted nuts from a plastic sack balanced between his thighs. It was his way of reclaiming his virility.

She rushed to his side like he was the last man on earth. Dawson held up his hand. "Not too close, Cece. I've got the flu. I don't want to give it to you. Damn, you look fantastic. It's great to see you. I've missed you. I can't thank you enough for coming."

"The flu?"

"Yeah, and that's not all I've got. I've got a whole lotta loving in my heart and I'm saving it just for you."

"The flu is curable. But you, well I'm not so sure there is a cure," she teased. "When you're well enough to get it up, I'll take care of all that lovin in your heart. Now, you get some rest and maybe we can have breakfast together tomorrow morning. I assume you reserved an apartment for me."

"Yup. The same one, right next to mine. The door is open. The key is on the kitchen counter. Thanks again for coming. Considering what's going on in Port Moresby, this is probably the safest place for both of us. I've got some ideas and need your input. We'll talk tomorrow."

"Get well, lover boy," she said while blowing a kiss in his direction. "Thanks for saving my ass. If it weren't for you, I probably would have died in the Hyatt."

CHAPTER ELEVEN

Doctor Quinn McDermott had taken control of Tony's care since his arrival – three to four visits a day, for going on eight weeks. While he was on the ventilator, she sat with him for hours, watching, praying, hoping to discover a clue as to how he survived. To her amazement, Tony's condition improved every day. When he opened his eyes for the first time, he smiled at her and reached for her gloved hand as if he had somehow known she had nursed him back from the brink and wished to thank her for her diligent care and compassion. Shortly after she removed the ventilator tube, he sprang out of bed and commenced to do jumping jacks, push-ups, squats, leg lifts, sit-ups, and deep knee bends and spun around his room like a gymnast while Quinn laughed uncontrollably at his antics.

Quinn spent more time with Tony than any other woman he had ever met. He knew it and she knew it. And now that he was no longer attached to the incubator tube, they spent many hours talking, sharing family history, likes and dislikes, goals, and the reasons they wound up in PNG. They also shared what they planned to do if, and when, they ever made it home. Their encounters were quite professional and strictly platonic, at least that's how it started. Level-four protocol required her to remain dressed in her hazmat suit while she was with Tony. Nevertheless, Quinn would show up each morning with his breakfast, usually scrambled eggs, sausage, toast, and a hot cup of coffee. While she checked his vitals and drew a sample of his blood, he imagined she would look much more fetching in a bikini... or less.

She usually arrived with his evening meal around six and while he was eating, she summarized the current situation with Lucifer, citing the number of deaths, new outbreaks, and prophetic speculations from the CDC, WHO, NIH, Wall Street pundits, and politicians. No one seemed to have any good news. In fact, most of the pundits described a world without hope.

With no cure in sight, their conversations segued to their innermost feelings about the Almighty and how the world might end. Despite the dystopian future they faced, Tony made her feel warm inside. He made her laugh. She shared her innermost secrets. He told her stories. She let him into her heart.

Nevertheless, the pandemic remained front and center. Most conversations began with a "what's the latest body count?" or "have they found a cure?" Quinn did her best to stay abreast of the progress, or lack thereof.

Quinn keyed in the proper digital access code and entered Tony's room. "Good morning, Tony. How are you?" she asked, flashing her deep blue eyes.

"Good morning, sunshine. If it weren't for all these electrodes and needles, I'd jump out of bed and give you a big, wet kiss on your plastic faceplate. You look sooo sexy in that astronaut suit. How's life on the backside of the moon?"

"Not good. In fact, quite depressing. There's been fresh outbreaks in Port Moresby, Jakarta, Darwin, Sydney, some Asian countries. There are even fresh reports out of China. They usually don't say anything. But the worst of it is still in PNG. There are daily outbreaks in the highlands and along the rivers. Entire villages have been wiped out, two, three, even four hundred men, women, and children. The death toll in PNG is now over six thousand. Globally, CDC estimates as many as two hundred thousand. They're still looking at it under a microscope trying to understand how it works, why it attacks humans and no other primates or air breathing animals. It's an enigma."

"I'm sorry I asked." Tony shook his head and took a deep breath. The notion that he had some responsibility for this calamity burned a hole in his soul. Quinn sensed his remorse and touched his hand.

He'd become accustomed to her touch, even though she wore rubber gloves. "I guess Hemmingway is up to her neck in cremation ops."

"Oh, yeah. PNG is on lockdown. Airports are closed. Schools and businesses are closing. There's a shortage of food and drinking water. Power outages. Chaos in the city streets. It's fucking ugly, excuse my language, but that is how it is. If this continues at the current pace, Port Moresby will be doomed. It will be every man for himself, and I don't mean that metaphorically. Yeah, Hemmingway and her teams have been busy."

"Well, we're still kickin, so what's for dinner?"

Quinn giggled. "I've got some good news. You're going to be discharged soon. They've got an apartment for you, down the hall from Dawson and his girlfriend. And a few doors from mine."

"Mmm. Maybe we can have dinner at your place sometime soon."

"I make a mean pot of spaghetti."

"Yummy. I can't wait. Until then, I'm here to help. Are you going to put more holes in my arm?"

"No, not today. But I want to ask you a few questions about allergies. Are you allergic to cats?"

"No. I grew up with several pet cats. My favorite was Blackjack. He was a big tommy with golden eyes. He slept most of the day and chased mice at night. We were friends. A pack of coyotes took him from me one summer night. He was my last cat."

"That's awful. I'm sorry. What about ragweed, sage, or black walnut?"

"Nope. Never."

"Crab, shrimp, lobster, shellfish? Peanuts?"

"Are you kidding? I love seafood. And I've consumed thousands of peanuts while watching football."

"Alcohol, drugs?"

"I never used drugs or smoked. I drink on special occasions." Tony sensed Quinn was nervous, an emotion she had not displayed since their first few meetings. "How are you doing? You seem a bit nervous?"

Quinn began to cry. "I'm scared, really scared. You're the only person we know who has survived Lucifer. More than anything, you need to stay healthy. Otherwise, we may never be able to develop a vaccine or cure... and we... I mean you and I... well... there won't be any you and I."

"Hey, don't do this. Don't let it get to you. You've taken good care of me all these weeks, and I'll do my very best to keep us both safe. You've given me lots of great reasons to stay alive."

"Right now, we have no idea how to control it," she babbled. "It's grown into a global pandemic. Hundreds of thousands of people have died. Just like you, the first symptoms are flu-like, but it kills quickly. We're doing our best, but it is spreading fast."

Tony was not afraid of dying and certainly didn't wish to become a martyr. He simply wanted to make a difference and spend more time with Quinn.

"You're a courageous man. Listen, I need to tell you something. It's top secret but you need to know. Besides, what are they gonna do? Throw me in jail? So, here's the facts. I do not work for CDC. I work for NASA. My official title is Principal Investigator for the Invasive Species Group."

Tony's eyebrows rose high on his wrinkled forehead.

"Dawson is the only other person from Keystone that knows about this. He was briefed the day we arrived. A few years ago, NASA launched a manned mission to Mars to retrieve a core sample that one of our rovers drilled from an iron meteor. The rover's remote sensing devices indicated the presence of organic material in the core sample. It turned out to be Lucifer, but the astronauts didn't know how dangerous it was. Even though they were fully protected in EVA suits, they became infected. Maybe they took off their helmets or had a leak in their suit." Quinn choked and her eyes filled with tears. "They died on Mars, a man and a woman. They made a video of their deaths and transmitted it to Houston. It's very graphic."

Her sobs and heavy breathing momentarily fogged her plastic faceplate. Unable to wipe her eyes, she lifted her head high, smiled and regained a veneer of resilience. "It is – what it is." Quinn shrugged her slender shoulders and took another deep breath. Her eyes focused on his, penetrating deep into his consciousness, mustering every joule of optical communication energy while whispering, "I love you."

CHAPTER TWELVE

Like the first rumblings of an imminent earthquake, the sharp salvos of automatic weapons fire, combined with the earsplitting blast from an RPG, startled everyone in the entire Keystone facility.

Dawson quickly slipped on his boots and grabbed his walkie-talkie, Glock 21, and a shoulder holster containing six clips of ammunition and a small can of mosquito spray. When he reached the elevator, the door was closed. He pushed the button and waited impatiently. "Come on. Come on!" he shouted. While waiting, he was joined by Hemmingway, three members of Hemmingway's unit, and Cece. Hemmingway shouldered a Remington Hi-Power. Her team carried assault rifles. Cece arrived in her see-through nightie armed with a steak knife.

"Cece. No need for you to be here." Dawson couldn't help but chuckle. "Sweetie, we'll see what's going on. Please go back to your apartment. Make us some coffee. I'll be back shortly. I'm sure our security team, plus Doctor Hemmingway and her troops can handle this. Go on, now. You're not dressed…"

The elevator door opened and everyone, except Cece, boarded.

As soon as they reached the ground floor Dawson keyed the security chief. "This is Dawson. What's happening?"

"This is Lieutenant Fletcher. There were ten infiltrators – natives from Wabag area. They needed some food. There are no injuries. They blew up a rock with an RPG. Made a lot of noise, but no harm done. We've contained the insurgents and will provide them some food in exchange for their weapons. The party is over. Everyone can go back to bed."

"Thanks, LT. Will do. You heard the man. Back to nighty-night."

"I have a feeling this won't be the last raid," Hemmingway opined. "This is exactly how it started in Africa during the Ebola pandemics. A few disgruntled natives at first, but two nights later we were attacked by a much larger force – fifty or sixty armed and desperate men. Fletcher knows how to deal with these problems and his men have considerably more firepower. Unless they come at us with armored vehicles and something larger than an AK-47 or RPG, we're well protected."

Hemmingway recalled the tragic events she and her team encountered during the African Ebola pandemics. Desperate people will do desperate things.

*****

Shortly after the fireworks, Rachel microwaved a cup of instant coffee, walked to her deck overlooking the pit and called David.

"David, this is Rachel."

"Hello, Rachel. What's the latest from Keystone?"

"We have a problem – just like Africa. We're going to need more security. I have a gut feeling Keystone may soon be under siege."

"I can spare a few men, but we have a much larger crisis on our hands here in Port Moresby. But first, I want to tell you what our metallurgical guru discovered when he analyzed the metal from the core that contained the Lucifer organism."

"Shucks, I almost forgot about the core sample. I recall, it was about ten feet long, with the Lucifer organism sandwiched between two sections of an iron meteor. That's the same configuration the NASA rover discovered on Mars."

"Yup, that's the one. You may want to sit down. This is a shocking development. Our lab engineer performed a standard XRF alloy diffraction analysis of the metal surrounding Lucifer. We know it was iron based due to magnetism and the XRF fluorescence confirmed it. What we didn't know was the iron was alloyed with other metals... to make it more heat resistant. Are you following me?"

"You're beginning to scare the crap outta me."

"This alloying process was not something Mother Nature could do. It could only be created by intelligent beings or highly advanced AI controlled robots – at least as intelligent as we humans are today."

"My God, this is really creepy. Why didn't we figure that out with the Mars sample?"

"We never brought the Mars core home, and the astronauts didn't have the metallurgical tools to conduct an elemental analysis. The Mars meteor was a relic from another galaxy and was probably billions of years old."

"I know all about panspermia events and the likelihood that early life forms, or the chemicals needed for life, arrived on earth billions of years ago on a comet, meteor or asteroid. What's so important about the metallurgy? Most iron meteors contain other elements, mostly nickel."

"Hold your horses, Hemmingway. There's more. While most iron meteors are alloyed with nickel, this iron meteor was alloyed with tungsten and carbon. Both these elements remain stable up to sixty-five hundred degrees Fahrenheit. Iron-nickel alloys melt at sixteen hundred. Therefore, much of the typical iron meteor would burn up as it traveled through our atmosphere. However, the addition of tungsten and carbon with iron would raise the melting temperature of the meteor to about five thousand degrees. In other words, the meteor was a vessel, a protective canister designed to travel through space – and penetrate an atmosphere as dense as ours – *without melting.*"

"That's incredible. Quinn and the others will freak out when they learn this."

David continued. "We, I mean NASA, has often wondered if something like this might happen. They even had some preliminary action plans. Funny, we've learned how to deal with Ebola, Marburg, HIV, multiple coronavirus mutations, and malaria. But something from outer space – specifically designed to be a natural born killer – something so outrageous and life-threatening as Lucifer… well, we're just not prepared. It's like the zombie movies. One thing leads to another, and another, and so on, until the end of humanity. Frankly, we're not prepared for this level of carnage. Port Moresby is dying. We're of no value here and are no closer to a solution than when we started. Am I repeating myself? It's not safe here. Warlords have taken over the food, medical, and drinking water supplies. We can't transport our recovery teams to the outbreaks. Thousands of bodies have been left to rot on the streets. Our last death count was over twelve thousand, but it's probably closer to twenty or thirty thousand by now. And we know it is rapidly spreading. CDC has reported several new outbreaks in other countries. We've got to get out of here, now. I'm going to transfer everything to Keystone. Like Georgie Custer said at the Battle of The Little Big Horn…we'll make our last stand there. Have you got room for about a hundred people?"

"Sure, we can handle everyone. There's the hotel and apartments. Take your pick. But, now more than ever, with all the additional people, we'll desperately need a reliable supply of food, water, level-four PPE, medical supplies – everything for my team and yours – about a hundred and sixty people. That's a lot of mouths to feed. We have an airstrip long enough for your C-5 Galaxy. Supplies can also be paradropped if necessary. We'd be better off if we were surrounded by real zombies. We could kill them from five hundred yards with sniper fire." Rachel momentarily snickered, then segued back to reality.

"The Highland Highway is not safe – too many roving gangs. Those fucking thieves will kill you for a candy bar. The only safe way in or out of Keystone is by air. We've got some choppers and a few small fixed wing aircraft. Do you need us to assist in your evacuation?"

"No. I don't believe that will be necessary. The toughest part for us is getting everything from our base of operations into the C-5. We have our own armed security and they're experienced in dealing with this type of insurrection. I'm going to bring all our lab instruments, power generation, global communication systems, food, fuel, and supplies – everything of value. We've got a few choppers so we should be able to ship le everything. And I've got a large stash of kina bills – enough to pay for a forklift to load our gear at the airport."

"David, make sure you alert Atlanta that we're going to need outside support for an indefinite period. We won't make much of a stand without it. We're gonna need regular shipments – reliable shipments. Dawson knows what we need and when. Food, diesel for the generators, trucks, and buses, propane for the mobile crematoriums plus level-four PPE, N95 respirators, and aviation fuel for the choppers. The list goes on."

"I'll do my best. But we need to consider the possibility Atlanta may not be able to fulfill our needs."

"Yeah, I know it's a long shot. Keep me posted on your ETA."

"Will do. Thanks, Rachel. Wish us luck. I'll call when we're airborne."

*****

Dressed in baby blue medical scrubs, Tony was watching a satellite news feed when two figures dressed in civilian attire appeared in the air lock. With a hissing shot of compressed air, the inner door swung open allowing Dawson and Quinn to enter his room.

"Good morning, Tony." Dawson exclaimed, wrapping his arms around his friend. They embraced as real men do, then backed off.

Quinn took his hand in hers and looked about the naked room. "Are you sure you want to leave this lovely place?" she joshed. "Cause if you do, I may not be able to bring you your meals, or give you a back rub, or read you a bedtime story."

Tony launched a grateful smile. "Maybe it's time for me to coddle you. Dawson, this young lady is a magician. She's a bonafide miracle worker. Look at my waistline – at least two inches bigger than when I first arrived. It's all Quinn's doing. She deserves a medal and a big raise."

The room was just as antiseptic and unattractive as it was ten weeks earlier. The spartan accommodations included an adjustable hospital bed, an instrument package containing a vital sign data processor, and a colorful flat-screen monitor. No longer connected to his head and arm, a collection of tubes and electrical wires wiggled and wound their way from here to there and somewhere under the crumpled white sheets of an empty bed. To the left of the bed, a small bathroom with a glistening commode, sink, and shower accompanied by the olfactory remnants of high-octane disinfectant. Upon closer inspection, one would observe a smoke detector hanging from the wall nearest the latrine while a single automatic sprinkler head stood guard duty from the ceiling.

Quinn dropped a duffle bag at Tony's feet. "I brought you some street clothes. Nothing fancy, some underwear, a pair of khaki shorts, a blue T-shirt, and a pair of flip-flops. I hope everything fits."

"Thank you, Quinn. You saved my life. I owe you big time."

Dawson picked up the beat. "I've got a couple, actually three things for you. First, your paycheck. Second, here's the key to your new apartment."

Quinn interrupted. "It's a few doors from mine." She winked. "Sorry, Dawson, I needed to get that off my chest, um, er… my mind," she chuckled.

"And finally…" Dawson handed Tony a letter. "It's a job offer. I need your help. There's too much turmoil around here for me to handle on my own. The job description, salary, hazard pay – it's all in that offer. I hope you'll accept it."

"Thanks, Dawson." A single teardrop appeared in each eye. "I'm very grateful for everything." He focused his attention on Quinn. "What do you want me to do?" he asked tenderly.

"Stay with me. I need you by my side."

"That's my gal. Okay, Dawson. You can count on me. What's the agenda?"

"Toss those scrubs, get dressed like you're alive, and let's have lunch. We've got a lot to talk about."

"What is the protocol for leaving this tomb?" Tony asked Quinn.

"Shower, shave, leave everything. Dress in your new duds and follow me."

CHAPTER THIRTEEN

Still steaming and dreaming in the effervescent afterglow of their first tryst, Quinn raised one eyelid at the sound of her shower. Tony was just stepping out from the spray with a large towel over his shoulder. She opened the other eye and watched him dry himself, turning his back to her, then his front. To Quinn, he was a masterpiece of manhood.

"Pssst. Hey, you!" she simpered. "Psst! Hey, manly man," she chirped with an Aussie accent.

Tony heard her bidding and felt her gaze. He turned full frontal and struck a bodybuilder's pose.

"Wow. Look at those muscles, and Mr. Dandy. Come to me, lover boy. We're not done – not by a long shot."

Knowing it was just a scintillating game of foreplay, he swaggered up to her bed and stood motionless while she admired his physique. Quinn threw back the covers, exposing her naked flesh. Then smiled invitingly, gently captured his manhood and slowly guided him into bed.

Meanwhile, three doors down the hall, a thin slice of the rising sun pierced through an opening in the shutters of the east-facing bedroom window. Dawson rubbed his sleepy eyes. Cece was snoring.

The lone sunbeam illuminated her exposed breast. Dawson leaned forward and kissed her half-open mouth. Was this his bed or hers? The question lingered, but it really didn't matter. She had fixed a delicious dinner – a ribeye steak with Spanish rice, sourdough rolls and an Italian red.

No matter how hard he tried, regardless of his pleadings, he knew they didn't share the same kind of love. Just as she had proclaimed on numerous occasions, she had a soft spot in her heart for him, but what kept her coming back was the sex, only the sex. Last night was no different. As soon as he began to tell her how much he loved her, she whisked him off to bed where they fucked like bunnies for thirty minutes and fell asleep in a puddle of carnal perspiration.

*****

"Wake up, lovebirds, time to earn your pay!" Rachel yelled after three whacks on Quinn's apartment door. Quinn quickly retrieved her bathrobe and opened the apartment door. Rachel greeted her with a penny-ante giggle, then looked at Tony sitting up in Quinn's bed. "We've got a hot outbreak in the rainforest. Wabag police called it in. One of their river patrols found it yesterday – Jaba river village – Smaark tribe – upwards of two hundred people."

Rachel looked over Quinn's shoulder and raised her voice. "Hi, Tony. Nice to see that you've fully recovered and are just as charming as ever. I thought you might want to join us. I expect the scene will be alarming, so if you're not up to it… I'll understand."

"No, I want to see what we're dealing with. What do you want me to do?"

"Just watch and learn. You never know. Maybe it will trigger a new idea. Quinn and her team are still looking for a cure or vaccine and she'll soon have more people to help her. Our Port Moresby team is evacuating. They're coming here soon, about a hundred CDC personnel."

"What about Dawson?" asked Tony. "He might want to go. He visited that village – told us about the young Smaark man who found the gold nugget."

"I tried to call him a few minutes ago. He wasn't in his room."

"Try three doors down the hall. He's probably with his friend, Cece. She's a midnight wailer," Tony smirked.

Quinn rolled her eyes and shrugged her shoulders. "I'm going with you."

"Great. Meet up at the heliport in thirty minutes."

Rachel walked down the hall and knocked three times on Dawson's apartment door.

"Hold on. Gimme a second to put on some pants," Dawson yelled.

She could hear him stumbling toward the door and the clink of the deadbolt as it was disengaged.

"Good morning, Doctor. I thought I heard your voice down the hall. What's up?"

"I'm sorry, but there's been an outbreak reported along the Jaba river. It's the Smaark village. That's where you and your lady friend, Cece, visited awhile back."

Dawson shook his head in disbelief. "Goddamnit. I thought this might happen. When are you leaving?"

"Thirty minutes, heliport. You can bring your friend if you wish. Make sure she's dressed out properly in level-four attire and has the stomach for this. She's going to see lots of dead bodies and maybe some crocodiles."

"Will do. I'll join you and ask Cece if she wants to come. See you at the heliport."

Dawson closed the door and sat down on the bed. He placed his hand on Cece's arm and shook her until she awoke.

"What time is it?" she moaned, rubbing her eyes.

"Past seven. I've got to go. There's been another outbreak. I'm afraid it's the village we visited. You remember, Tatu, Bossman Tom, the Smaark tribesmen dressed in their ceremonial costumes – the men who greeted us with their penis gourds."

"Fuck, I'll never forget that. Their balls were showing." Cece chuckled. "Why do you have to go? I thought we could sleep in and maybe… you know…."

"I have to go. I've got to learn what happened to these people. They were my friends. I trusted them and they trusted me. Christ Almighty, one of them found the gold nugget that led us to Gemini Falls."

"Well, that didn't turn out so good, did it?" Her dark sarcasm took a bite out of his heart.

Feeling like he was holding the short end of the rope, Dawson continued. "Look, maybe this is not for you. It's going to be messy – dead bodies. You may not have the fortitude to see this. It might have happened to you if you had stayed in the bush any longer."

The word "fortitude" triggered her bravado. "When are we leaving?"

"Thirty minutes. I'll get us a couple of hazmat suits and coffee to go. You get up and do your five-minutes-and-out-the-door thingy. We'll dress in the chopper."

*****

When it was time to lead her team, Rachel was at her best.

"Dawson, I'm glad you and Cece could make it. You'll be in chopper one with me and half the recovery team. Tony, you and Quinn hop in chopper two with the rest of the recovery team. Chopper three has the mobile crematorium and the body-snatchers. We'll use it if the bodies are intact. However, if the crocs got to them, they'll be ripped to pieces – too much blood and guts. We may have to burn them in place with the exothermic cremation blankets."

With everyone strapped in, the helicopters sequentially lifted off the ground beginning with chopper one. Once airborne, the three helicopters quickly climbed through a low-lying layer of fog, before reaching their cruising altitude. Here the skies were crisp and blue, with puffs of nimbus clouds scattered across the sky.

Traveling in a north-westerly direction, the thirty-minute flight skirted the tallest mountain peaks in the central highlands – some over fourteen thousand feet. Upon reaching the Jaba river, they turned north and followed the muddy bank for another ten minutes until reaching the Smaark village.

As they crossed over a line of tall trees surrounding the village, Rachel shouted, "We've got crocs. Bastards are everywhere. Fire team, lock and load. Skipper, hover over the field of fire. My God, this is the worst. Fucking crocs have no mercy for the dead. Fire at will!"

Even as they were being massacred by a barrage of high-power assault weapons, the crocodiles continued to rip away at the limbs and bellies of the native bodies. As the fusillade intensified, crocodile heads and bellies exploded while the ravenous crocodiles broadcast mortal howls across the village grounds.

Upon seeing the bodies, a wave of nausea rose from Tony's stomach. He swallowed hard in his attempt to mentally suppress the revulsion. But the overwhelming power of so much death gave way to grotesque visions of Lenny and the rest of his crew lying on the ground.

"Are you okay?" Quinn yelled.

"I will be. Just need to clear my head. Go on, do your thing. I'll stay back and watch."

Rachel then ordered the helicopters to land. As the wheels of her chopper touched the ground, she began to make a mental tally of the body count. It seemed there were more arms and legs than matching bodies. She called for two members of her team to follow her down the central walkway into the village. The others were to fan out, dispatch any living or wounded crocodiles and count the bodies.

At the sight of the butchery, Cece was horror-stricken. Dizzy and unable to stand, she turned away from the open door, bent over at the waist and regurgitated a slurry of coffee, ribeye steak, Spanish rice, sourdough rolls and Italian red – *inside her hazmat suit.*

"I'm sorry, Cece." Dawson grabbed her arm and settled her into one of the seats. "Stay put. You'll be fine. Just don't open your suit. You can clean up when we get back to Keystone."

Cece coughed up a few bits and pieces, slumped back in her seat and closed her eyes.

Dawson tried to speak to her in a consoling tone. But she was in no mood to reply and waved him away. Rather than press the issue, he patted her on the shoulder and joined the recovery team.

Dawson couldn't believe the repulsive sight before him. He slowly navigated around the bodies of men, women, and children, looking for Tatu, Bossman Tom, and the other elders he and Cece had met on his first visit. "Twenty-one, twenty-two, twenty-three," he counted aloud.

Surprisingly, he found himself standing in front of the spirit house. Two carved hardwood spirit masks stood guard. The air was so quiet, he could hear the flies buzzing inside the structure, spinning aimlessly in willy-nilly patterns. He took a cautious first step, then another, and another until he was able to push open the woven grass and bamboo doorway.

Four bodies hung by their necks from the bamboo joists. He took a few steps forward, then stopped and gasped at their faces. The first was Bossman Tom, dressed in his celebration finery. His ceremonial koteka pointed to the heavens. A hand-woven rope was tied to the uppermost horizontal beam and coiled around his neck with a slip knot. Even though he was dead, the spear he had carried for decades remained clutched in his fist.

To his right hung Ram, the Marlboro man. He too was dressed in his ceremonial finery, including a bright yellow koteka and a wild pig tusk protruding from his nose.

Next came Yanun, the betelnut chewer. His neck was broken, his head unnaturally skewed to the left. An impressive necklace containing a large cassowary claw and numerous kina shells encircled his neck.

Lastly, Tatu. The rope cinched tightly around his slender neck. His necklace had been severed. His treasured cassowary claw and crocodile teeth were now scattered on the split bamboo floor. For a second, Dawson thought it might be appropriate to take a photograph of the ritual mass suicide, but he quickly changed his mind. This image was something only the Smaark people should share in their spiritual afterlife. He picked up the cassowary claw and kina shells and rolled them in his gloved fingers. For a moment, he felt a tug around his neck. "These belong to the Smaark spirits," he whispered. Then, as he was about to turn and leave, he saw a small piece of paper on the floor. It was a note from Tatu.

I am Tatu, I am with my brothers and sisters. Crocodiles will not eat my spirit.

*****

Rachel could hardly believe her eyes. She was dressed in khaki shorts, T-shirt and hiking boots. A large brimmed hat covered most of her blond hair. Her face and neck were draped in a large mosquito net. She was sitting on a sago drum, trembling. Rachel approached with caution.

"I'm here to help you," said Rachel softly. Please don't be afraid. I know this white suit looks funny. I promise, I'm here to help you."

Her eyes told a story of irrevocable terror. How she managed to survive was a complete mystery. But, like Tony, the fact that this young woman was alive foreshadowed the possibility for a cure.

"My name is Rachel. I'm a doctor and I'm here to help you. May I sit with you?"

The woman nodded but did not speak.

"I know what happened here. It was the mushrooms. Right?"

The woman nodded but did not speak.

"What is your name?"

The woman looked at Rachel. "Yvette. Yvette Michel."

"You speak English?"

"Yes, but I am from Biarritz, France."

"How long have you been here?"

The woman looked at Rachel but didn't speak. Her eyes were focused on a point in space toward the river.

"Did you come here by boat, a tour boat?"

"Yes, I am from Biarritz, France. My name is Yvette. I wanted to see the rainforest and meet the native people."

"I understand. Did you have any companions?"

Yvette nodded. "My boyfriend, Drew. He went into the river."

"Where is Drew now?"

Yvette looked at Rachel and began to sob. "He went into the river. He never came back. He left me here. Am I going to die? I don't want to die." Yvette buried her head in her hands and snuggled close to Rachel. After a few minutes, the young woman stopped crying and began to tell more of her plight.

"Drew and I were going to be married. We wanted to see the world. It was supposed to be a great adventure, exploring remote villages, meeting natives, something we would remember all our lives. But after we arrived, something happened. There were other tourists here. Some of them were sick, coughing, sneezing. The boat left us. The next day, most of the villagers were sick. I was sick too. Then, everyone started to die, and I saw the… mushrooms. I hid under one of the bamboo huts. Then the crocodiles came and.. oh, Drew… I miss you, mi amor."

"It's all right to cry for the people we love."

Rachel called out, "Quinn! Quinn, come to me. We have a survivor. Come quick. I'm behind the spirit house."

Quinn rushed toward Rachel's voice. As she rounded the spirit house, she saw Rachel and the survivor.

"Yvette, this is my friend, Doctor McDermott. She's going to help you – take you to a safe place. It is not far, by helicopter. It's okay. Go with Quinn. Okay?"

With tearful eyes, Yvette looked at Rachel and nodded.

"Her name is Yvette. She's in shock. She lost her fiancé. Get her settled in your helicopter and start a crystalloid IV. Stay with her while we finish up here."

Rachel walked back to the center of the village and called the recovery teams together for a briefing.

"What's the body count?" Rachel shouted.

One by one, the team leaders called out their findings.

"Sixty-two."

"Fifty-eight."

"Seventy-one."

"Sixty-five."

"Dawson was the last to share his observations. "There are four elders in the spirit house. They committed suicide – hanged themselves. I knew these men. One of them was Tatu. He's the young man who discovered the Gemini Falls gold nugget. He left a note saying he was afraid the crocodiles would eat him."

Rachel shook her head in dismay and exasperation. "Two hundred and sixty plus one unlucky Frenchman, who went for a swim and never returned makes the total two hundred and sixty-one. That's an absurd number. Lucifer is kicking our butts. However, I do have some good news. We have another survivor. She's a French tourist from Biarritz. She lost her fiancé, and she's going back to Keystone with us. I'm sure Quinn will take good care of her. Let's wrap this up. I'll call in the crematorium team. They'll take care of the bodies and burn the village."

*****

While Rachel and her team remained in the village assisting the cremation operations, Dawson returned to the helicopter to check on Cece.

"What the fuck are you up to?" Dawson screamed. "You were told to keep your hazmat suit on. Goddamnit, Cece!" An avalanche of panic roared into his heart.

Cece believed he was overreacting. "Why are you yelling at me? Can't you see I've been sick? I couldn't breathe. The smell was horrible. I couldn't tolerate the smell inside this fucking suit. I needed fresh air. What's the big fuckin deal?"

"Quick! Get back into your suit, and don't say a fucking thing."

"Okay, as usual, you've got to have it your way." Cece zipped up her hazmat suit, leaned back in her chair, crossed her arms over her chest, and began to sulk.

A wave of guilt boiled in Dawson's veins and he suddenly felt the sting of culpability. He held a deep sense of grief for Cece – something he would bear for the rest of his life. But Rachel had to know the truth.

"I told her to zip up her suit, and she did, but she was probably unprotected for at least an hour."

"You're fucking kidding," Rachel bellowed – her face turning chalky white as she weighed the ramifications of what Dawson had just disclosed.

"Is she fucking possessed? What the hell was she thinking?" Rachel was rightfully outraged. "She'll be quarantined for at least a week. We've got sixty people to protect – a hundred more when the Port Moresby team arrives. Goddamnit, Dawson, this is a life or death situation. We're not playing Marco Polo in the backyard pool. But you did the right thing. I know you care for Cece. Hopefully, she will be fine. We'll know by this time tomorrow."

CHAPTER FOURTEEN

Like a giant flying dragon, the roar of four turbofan engines rattled every window and coffee cup in the Keystone complex. With her flaps down, The C-5X Galaxy made a low-level pass over the lengthened Keystone runway, fluttering her massive wings to announce her arrival. As the massive aircraft crossed over the open pit, the pilot pushed the nose down and lowered the landing gear. No doubt, she was coming in heavy – every bit of her gross weight of eight hundred and sixty thousand pounds. The instant her twenty-eight wheels touched the pavement, a cloud of pungent white smoke exploded skyward. The pilot pushed the engines into reverse thrust, causing a whirlwind of dust to blow into the sky, and slowly brought the beast to a crawl. Her immense wingspan of two hundred and fifty feet, and similar fuselage length, duly impressed those who witnessed the arrival.

As the winged monster taxied toward the terminal, three helicopters landed sequentially at the designated tarmac. David Stockton was the first to disembark. Rachel and Dawson were there to greet him.

"Welcome to Keystone, David." Rachel and David punched knuckles.

"It's good to see you, Rachel. You look superlative as usual." Turning to Dawson, he introduced himself. "Hi, I'm David Stockton. You must be Dawson Elliott. Rachel has told me about you. All five stars. Glad to have you on our team. I'd like you to meet Doctor Jonah Sweet. He led our Port Moresby mycotic disease research lab. Unfortunately, we didn't have any survivors, so his work was limited to autopsies."

"It's a pleasure to meet you both," replied Dawson. "You've made an impressive arrival. I have arranged for fork-lifts and trucks per your request. There's plenty of secure storage for your equipment and supplies. We've reserved living quarters per your instructions."

"Great. My logistics supervisor, Jack Thomas, looks forward to working with you and your team. Thanks for sending us a map of your facilities. The duality of this place is interesting – once the biggest gold mine in the world… and now a fortified citadel for fighting an unknown biological enemy from outer space. That has kind of a surreal appeal."

"Let's walk to our conference room. We have much to discuss. We all want to hear what's going on in Port Moresby and the rest of the world. And we'll bring you up to date on our operations," said Rachel.

"That would be great," David said, checking the time on his watch.

*****

Feeling somewhat out of place, Dawson led the entourage of scientists to the conference room where Doctors David Stockton, Rachel Hemmingway, Quinn McDermott, Phillip Jenkins, and Jonah Sweet were seated. Everyone was anxious to share information they had acquired since the death of Lenny.

David sat at the head of the long table and was the first to speak.

"We had no choice. Port Moresby was in turmoil. The Army had roadblocks on all major access roads including the Highland Highway. All rail, marine, and commercial airlines are on lockdown. No flights in or out. To my knowledge, there are no Americans in PNG except those of us here in Keystone or who refused to leave for an assortment of reasons. The government initiated a six p.m. to six a.m. curfew, which unfortunately is not being enforced. The Prime Minister has declared a national emergency and martial law. Rioters and looters are being shot in the act. Anyone caught attempting to escape quarantine is shot. We placed a couple of mobile propane crematoriums in the parking lot with instructions on how to use them. Nevertheless, the locals are burning bodies in the streets. It's chaos everywhere with thousands of men, women, and children in panic mode – plus gangsters roaming the downtown streets." David took a sip of coffee and inhaled a few deep breaths.

"I have some casualty numbers from the local authorities plus our own estimates based on the most recent field data. But because this is such a rapidly deteriorating situation, I suspect these figures don't reflect the full extent of the casualties. Greater Port Moresby has a population of about five hundred thousand people. Some of the outlying areas have reported body counts in excess of forty percent. Other reports, near the town center, are about sixty percent. Coupled with our own data, I would estimate the death toll to be about two hundred thousand."

"Two hundred thousand... in Port Moresby?" Rachel repeated David's estimate with an incredulous frown.

"And rapidly climbing." David exchanged an impassioned glance with the group. "The number is growing exponentially. A week or two from now, it could be... close to a hundred percent – *five hundred thousand people -- the entire population of Port Moresby.*" David choked on his last words.

Rachel shook her head, knowing her wishes would never come true. "What's going on in America, Canada, Europe, China, Africa?

We've not been able to get accurate data from the internet. I suspect the reports are sugar coated."

"I agree the information is sketchy and possibly invalid. The CDC, WHO and NIH numbers don't match up either. So, I understand your skepticism. As for the United States, there have been numerous outbreaks in most of the major cities including LA, San Francisco, Dallas, Miami, Chicago, New York, DC, and others. Homeless encampments are decimated as are old-age care facilities. I don't have accurate data, but my gut tells me the numbers are in the tens of thousands. As expected, China is mum, so it's anyone's guess. Southeast Asia, including Australia, New Zealand, Indonesia, Singapore, Malaysia, Philippines, Thailand, and South Korea, have all reported dozens of outbreaks. But I don't have any casualty figures, probably because the incubation period is so short and as a result the number of deaths is growing exponentially. A rough estimate would be five to ten percent of the population has died or will die in the next few weeks. We desperately need accurate death rate models. We know these numbers are exponential, but we don't have enough reliable input data or a viable algorithm. God knows, I wish I had better news. There are no commercial flights, cruise or cargo shipping anywhere in the world. Each country is dealing with their own problems. Thanks to greedy hoarders, food and drinking water supplies are rapidly declining in many metropolitan areas. People living in third-world countries are starving to death while the warlords take control of emergency UN food and water supplies and are literally making a killing."

Rachel suspended the grisly news. "Let's take a short break and try to flush the morbidity from our brains. I need to take a pee and grab a coffee. We'll reconvene in twenty minutes."

Dawson approached Rachel while she poured herself a cup of coffee. He was wearing the face of a broken man. "I just received a text message from ICU. Cece is… she didn't make it. I've got to leave. I might be late for the next session."

"I'm so sorry, Dawson. It breaks my heart to lose anyone. She was a special person. I know she meant a lot to you. Don't worry about the briefing. You and I… we can talk later."

*****

Dawson rushed to the ICU where he was greeted by the lead nurse.

"I'm sorry she's gone, Mr. Elliott. We did our best to keep her comfortable. She was ventilated on pure oxygen. Doctor McDermott tried every antifungal. She just didn't respond. She did not suffer. She wanted morphine – and we gave her what she wanted."

"May I see her?"

"She's extremely infectious. You can look at her through the window, but if you need to enter her room, you'll need to put on level-four gear."

Dressed in a hazmat suit, Dawson passed through the air lock and approached her corpse. A white sheet was pulled over her body. "Goddamnit, why didn't you listen? We could have been a couple. We could have shared a life. I wanted to be your partner forever." Mournful tears welled up in the corners of his eyes, raced down his cheeks and pooled in the corners of his lips. He reflected on the unforgettable moments they had shared. Licking the salty streams from his mouth he said, "Goodbye, Cece. See you on the other side."

As he was about to leave, he noticed a swelling in the fabric covering her face. He knew what it was but was driven to remove the sheet. As he exposed her face, the bright red dome of a Lucifer mushroom sprouted from her gaping mouth.

*****

Meanwhile, everyone except Dawson had returned to the briefing.

Rachel brought the meeting back to the task at hand. "Let's switch gears and talk about our operations here at Keystone. Quinn, you have some good news to report, so let's hear all about it."

Quinn stood to face her audience. "Our first survivor, Tony Esperanza, has fully recovered. In fact, he and I have been working together to make sure our second survivor, a young Frenchwoman named Yvette Michel, has the same good fortune."

David choked on the pen he was nervously chewing. "A second survivor! That's sensational news." He leaned forward, anxious to harvest the details.

"We found her two days ago during a village sweep. Everyone else was dead – two hundred and sixty villagers and one French tourist, who happened to be Yvette's fiancé."

"Don't forget to mention the crocs," noted Rachel.

"Crocodiles – the monsters of the rainforest. If the infected village is near a river, we must deal with some very ravenous crocodiles. I believe they attack the casualties within hours, so I would not be surprised to learn they also attack some living villagers as well. They have a special sense for death. We shoot as many as we can and leave them for the scavengers. It's the most gruesome part of our job."

David grimaced, then asked a more meaningful question. "Let's talk about how we plan to protect the living. What have you learned from the survivors?"

"Tony is from San Sebastian, Spain. Yvette is from Biarritz, France. Their immune systems are at the top of the charts. That may be the only reason they survived. We've done dozens of other tests, respiratory, blood tests, bone marrow, spleen, lymph nodes – immunoglobulin lg series – everything associated with the immune system. We didn't find any anomalies that would set them apart from the casualties. The only drugs we administered were standard antifungals, polyene and echinocandin."

"Have you compared any evolutionary or reproductive characteristics of Lucifer to other fungi? Seen any similarities?" asked David.

"Here's what we know. While Lucifer exhibits many characteristics of the typical asexual fungi we find on earth – it is not from earth. It came from some other place in the universe. Based on the metallurgical data CDC provided, it was likely packaged by an intelligent entity billions of years ago and was either launched into space or was ejected by a significant impact event – an intergalactic collision comes to mind. While trapped inside the metallic containment vessel, it remained in a state of anhydrobiosis – locked inside an iron container without water or nutrients, unable to metabolize. Who knows how long, or what happened to it while traveling through outer space, exposed to sub-freezing temperatures, supernova explosions and high levels of electromagnetic radiation. Despite these environmental conditions, the high temperatures passing through our atmosphere and incredible G-forces on impact with earth, it remained viable. In other words, it survived every possible hazard deep space could deliver and a fifty-thousand-mile-per-hour head-on-collision with our planet. Ooops, I almost forgot. After crashing into earth, it remained buried under billions of tons of dirt and rocks for another few hundred million years."

David interjected. "Hold that thought about anhydrobiosis. It's just one of many metabolic states. Fortunately, it is the most widely studied form of cryptobiosis where an organism reacts to adverse environmental conditions and shuts down all measurable metabolic processes indefinitely until hospitable conditions reappear. Tardigrades are one example. They can live without water for centuries – even in outer space. One or two drops of water and they come back to life. That's exactly what Lucifer did. That may, or may not be, coincidental. Maybe there's a clue somewhere in the DNA."

"We clearly need a breakthrough," said Quinn. "There are at least six known fungi here on earth, whose spores are deadly to humans.

Two of them live in the rainforests of PNG. But their victims die from respiratory pneumonia. Lucifer grows mycelia inside the lungs – like spaghetti. Death is by asphyxiation."

David acknowledged Quinn's assessment and continued to probe for more information. "I understand some PNG victims may have committed suicide. We've both found bodies lying face down on wet or muddy ground."

Quinn replied, "I don't think Lucifer victims intentionally commit suicide. Like Cordyceps, I think the victims are mind-driven to find a suitable place for the mushroom to reproduce. I'm quite sure Lucifer mushrooms excrete a similar psychotropic, mind-controlling chemical – a bioactive compound that interferes with the victim's nervous system and takes control of muscular movement shortly before death. Many Cordyceps species are host specific. It's Mother Nature's way of maintaining ecosystem balance. On the flip side, some host species have developed social immune techniques such as chemical warnings and formic acid disinfection. We're looking at these as possible vaccine options."

"How is that progressing?" asked Jonah.

"Not fast enough. We do the best we can with what we've got. Before you arrived, it was just Doctor Jenkins and me. We're delighted you joined our research effort. We don't have access to all the fungi species, but we are fortunate to have a genomic DNA system and cryo-electron microscope. There are over four hundred species of Cordyceps. Some chemically drill through the exoskeleton of their host – then consume their innards until they sprout a mushroom, usually from the head, and release fresh spores. Others invade the lungs, abdomen, or heart. The wind helps disperse the micron-size spores – some drift thousands of miles. That's the most troubling aspect. Damn spores from PNG can wind up just about anywhere on the planet – China, for example."

"That might be a good thing. Just kidding," snapped David. "I understand why you burn some of the bodies in place using exothermic cremation blankets. That's an approved CDC process. But what about the mycelia? Does the thermal blanket kill the mycelia? They may have grown into the wet soil and be somewhat insulated from the heat."

The room was suddenly haunted by five terrified faces.

"Fuck me!" Rachel mumbled. "I never thought about the mycelia."

"Nor did I," gasped Quinn.

Everyone slumped in their chair while they considered the dire implications. David brought them back from the depths of dread. "I don't believe Keystone is a high-risk area. Recall that I said we should hold the thought about anhydrobiosis. Lucifer is like any other fungi. While its sole purpose for living is to reproduce, it must have both water and nutrients. The rainforest provides all the water and nutrients it needs, so I would not be surprised if you found viable Lucifer mycelia growing in the rainforest where you burned the bodies. By contrast, Keystone is a massive rock quarry. There's nary a weed or rotten timber – nothing organic or nutritional. And while there may be puddles of standing water after a downpour, they're probably loaded with cyanide and other toxins from twenty years of processing gold-bearing ore. That said, we should see if there are any Lucifer mushrooms growing where you used exothermal blankets in the rainforest."

"Fuck! For a moment I thought... we... never mind," Rachel exhaled a sigh of relief while others silently thanked their Almighty for a chance at living. "We'll check out the places we used exothermic blankets and report the results."

*****

Dawson returned to the conference room, graciously accepted condolences from everyone and took his seat. Doing his best to put the loss of Cece behind him, he displayed the determination of a man facing ominous responsibilities.

"Is this an appropriate time to discuss logistics?" Dawson asked, looking at David. "We're going to need a reliable supply chain. What can CDC provide?"

"The USS *Kennedy*, the largest nuclear-powered aircraft carrier in the world, and other ships of U.S. Navy's seventh fleet, will provide logistical support for all CDC operations in the Pacific. With seventy ships, including ten nuclear subs, three hundred aircraft and over fifty thousand sailors and Marines, I think we'll be in good hands. We have a direct line to the *Kennedy*. You let me know what and when you need something, and I'll do my best to get it. As of this moment, we're the only CDC outpost they will serve."

Shaken by David's response, Rachel dared a question. "Are we the only CDC team in the Pacific working on the Lucifer problem?"

"Geographically speaking, yes, but CDC is planning to open another research center in Nevada at Area 51. Atlanta is well staffed, and we have research groups in London, the Atacama desert in Chile, and another in Dubai. The Chinese and Russians have initiated a co-operative effort in the Gobi Desert. The environmental conditions are perfect, but their location severely limits their resupply capabilities."

"Fuck, we might as well be on the backside of the fucking moon." Rachel relied on f-bombs to articulate her fears and frustrations.

CHAPTER FIFTEEN

Rachel had grown fond of the rainforest. Its beauty, diversity, grace, and challenges were just a few of the reasons she volunteered to take the PNG assignment. She adored and respected the native people, their culture and history. The thought of losing them to an organism as primordial as a mushroom was deeply disturbing.

Determined to know if Lucifer mycelia had invaded the rainforest, Rachel asked Dawson to schedule an aerial survey of the Gemini Falls core drilling site.

"No problem. Do you want a fly-over or your boots on the ground?" he asked.

"Jonah is joining us. He needs to see what we're dealing with in the rainforest. Let's do a fly-over first, and if it looks safe, then we can land. It's been about two months since we burned the bodies in place. Dress in level-four gear and bring a shovel."

*****

The Keystone chopper approached the Gemini Falls drill site from the south, then hovered about one hundred feet above the ground. What they observed shocked their senses.

"Goddamnit. Those red fuckers have found a new home!" Rachel shouted. "Look! Son of a bitch. Lucifer mushrooms are everywhere we burned a body with an exothermic blanket. This is hard to believe. Fifteen hundred degrees and these organisms are still viable. If I hadn't seen it first-hand, I would have said it was impossible. It's probably like this at every recovery site where we've used the blankets. How are we going to stop them? Jesus Christ. What a fucking disaster."

Jonah was speechless – his hopes and aspirations for a speedy resolution to this global pandemic were crushed. It wasn't like this in Port Moresby, or maybe it was, and he just hadn't seen it before evacuating the capital city for the security of Keystone.

Dawson took it all in stride, wrapped his arm around Rachel's shoulder and whispered, "It is what it is. Shit happens. I trust you'll find a way to deal with it. We all do."

*****

Dressed in his hazmat attire, Tony brought Yvette her breakfast, while Quinn checked her vitals.

"I see they have removed the incubation tube. How do you feel?" Tony asked.

"Bien. I'm good. No pain. Breathing is normal."

"I understand you are from Biarritz. That's Basque country. Parlez-vous l'euskara? Can you speak Basque language?"

"Un peu. A little."

"Parle-moi en euskara. Talk to me in Basque."

"Euskerrick asko gesaltzeagatik."

Tony was stumped. "You speak Basque much better than I."

"I said, thank you for my breakfast."

Quinn overhead the conversation and was puzzled. "What language are you speaking? I understood the French, but what was the other language?"

Tony was quick to reply. "Euskara. Basque. We're both from the Basque area. I'm from San Sebastian, Spain. Yvette is from Biarritz, France. We're neighbors – about thirty miles apart on the Bay of Biscay. It's one of the most beautiful places in the world. Very seductive. Quinn, you and I should go there someday. It's the most romantic location on the planet. I guarantee you'll fall in love with the place – and the Basque people will welcome you into their hearts."

"I know very little about that area or the people. I once read that Basque people are very healthy – they outlive all other races by seven or eight years. Is that true? Maybe it's the wine," Quinn chuckled.

"The wine is good, but longevity is in our blood. Basque people are famous for being Rh negative – forty percent or more. Asian, African, East Indian, North American and most others are Rh positive. Some northern European, Celts and Scots and their American descendants are also negative, but no more than fifteen percent. So, we're quite a novelty. Rh negative is the rarest blood type. Some people believe Rh negative people are the offspring of males from another planet who mated with human females." Tony snickered. "Nutty conspiracy theory, eh?"

Yvette was quick to add her perspective. "Tony, it's not funny. The alien theory is compelling, but there are other theories too. One theological notion is that Adam and Eve had negative blood. Another came from the Book of Enoch – the Nephilim descended from the heavens and mated with humans, creating a human-angel hybrid with Rh negative blood. Another theory is the extraterrestrial race called Anunnaki crossbred with humans. Regardless of where we came from, Rh negative blood is considered the purest blood on earth. Scientists can replicate Rh positive blood but have yet to replicate Rh negative."

"That is really fascinating." Quinn snuggled up to Tony. "Now I know why you're so smart, strong and handsome. Maybe I should include Rh negative blood in my Lucifer research. It may provide a clue as to how you and Yvette survived."

"That's a good idea," Yvette exclaimed. "You might discover why Rh negative people are resistant to malaria, toxoplasmosis, and many other parasites."

"Where did you guys learn these fascinating tidbits about Rh negative people?" asked Quinn.

"My parents, at school, and the Internet," replied Tony.

"Me too. We were taught to be proud of our Basque heritage – even if it's mysterious," replied Yvette.

*****

Rachel had taken a sip of wine and was just about to take a bite of her grilled ham and cheese sandwich when her smartphone chimed.

"Hi, Dawson. You caught me having dinner. Wanna join me?"

"Thanks, but I'm not hungry."

"Then, come help me drink a bottle of Cab."

"Now you're talkin my language. See ya in thirty seconds."

"The door is unlocked."

Dawson announced his arrival with a pair of knuckle taps on Rachel's door and entered her apartment.

"I'm in the living room. I've already filled your glass. My guess is you want something."

Shaking his head, Dawson smiled. "Good guess. Listen, my mind has been trying to make some sense of the iron meteor that we accidentally cored. For lack of a more scientific name, I call it the Lucifer starship. The metallurgical tests indicated it was manufactured by an intelligent entity at least as intelligent as twentieth century homo sapiens. Regrettably, we cored a small sample of it, causing the release of Lucifer. But, what does this intergalactic iron spaceship really look like? How big is it, and what other features might it have? I think we should conduct an aerial survey of the Gemini Falls drill site using ground-penetrating radar and whatever else may produce a sub-surface image. Who knows what we'll find?"

Rachel briefly raised a doubtful brow, but her expression rapidly segued to a wide grin. "When are we leaving?"

*****

The chopper slowly circled the Gemini Falls core site while Dawson operated a suite of sub-surface geological survey instrumentation – not an easy task from inside a bulky hazmat suit. His laptop was ablaze with multiple split-screen images, each depicting the digital interpretation of different electromagnetic frequencies and magnetic pulses. Like searching for a long-lost Mayan village now covered in three hundred feet of mud, rocks and lava, the survey data began to create a reproduction of the iron meteor.

As the pixels began to populate his computer, Dawson began to perspire with nerve-wracking anticipation. His hands trembled as he zoomed closer to the pixelating image emerging on his laptop screen. As soon as the two-dimensional version was complete, he switched to the three-dimensional mode. Seconds later, he gasped at the digital reproduction… then took a deep breath and began to rotate the image at various angles.

"What the hell is that thing?" asked Dawson.

Shocked and sweaty, Rachel cried out. "Unfuckingbelievable! You were right to call it the Lucifer starship, even if it sounds juvenile. How big is it? Pull up the ruler."

"My, oh my. This bad boy is almost twenty feet long… and about six feet in diameter. It's symmetrical too. And there's perfect hemispheres at both ends. It looks like a large propane storage tank."

"Could it be some kind of a fuel cell… maybe a bomb?" Rachel sputtered.

"I doubt it, but who really knows. Let's head home. I've got all the data we're gonna get with this equipment."

CHAPTER SIXTEEN

Exasperated, Quinn pulled away from the microscope.

"Damn!" she bellowed. "Jonah, please look at this polyene-treated cellular sample. Tell me what you think our next steps should be."

Jonah slid his chair a few feet and carefully focused the lens for optimum clarity.

"Duration of exposure?" he asked.

"Forty-eight hours. That's pushing the incubation period to the limit. Most victims will be dead by then. I saw some positive reaction early, but nothing after twelve hours. I've only got a few more drugs to try – some experimental antimycotics recently developed by CDC in Atlanta – the ones we received from the *Kennedy* a couple of days ago."

Jonah spoke while inspecting the sample. "Polyene works by binding to steroids inside the cell membrane. If it is successful, it literally desiccates the organism, removes most of the moisture and it dies. This sample looks like it was partially dehydrated, but with our high humidity, it was able to re-hydrate to stay viable. I think you should classify this as 'unlikely' and move on to the other antimycotics."

"Sounds like a plan. But first, I'm going to try the modified version of hydroxychloroquine – the malaria drug we've used for many years to treat outbreaks of coronavirus. It suppressed the bad proteins, those that caused respiratory inflammation and led to fatal viral pneumonia. Who knows? It may not cure the patient, but it may extend the incubation period and give us, and the patient, more time to recover. Have you tried the new antiviral?"

"Still incubating – won't know for another twelve hours. After you test chloroquine, I suggest you try allylamine. It was formulated to inhibit the cell from creating ergosterol. Like oxygen is needed for animals, single cell organisms cannot live without it. I know it's not easy – all these dead ends. Don't be flustered. Stay the course. Look on the bright side."

"The bright side?"

"You're never going to run out of Lucifer cells to play with."

"That's not funny."

*****

Rachel had just poured her first cup of coffee when there came a knock on her door.

"It's not locked. Whoever it is, come on in and join me for coffee," she shouted.

David opened her door. His face foretold bad news. Dawson was standing behind him, equally dismayed.

"I just finished a long conversation with the CDC guys on the USS *Kennedy*. I brought Dawson. He knows some of it but needs to hear the whole story."

"Grab some coffee. Let's sit in the living room."

Both men poured themselves a cup of coffee and walked into Rachel's living room. Dawson sat on one end of the couch. Rachel sat on the other. David slumped onto the lone sofa chair.

David began the conversation. "First I want to bring you up to date on the latest CDC data. This information was relayed to me via the CDC on the USS *Kennedy*. Lucifer is now classified as a category five outbreak on the global fungal pandemic index with PNG being the epicenter. More specifically, Enga province. None of us should be surprised by that declaration."

"Duhhh. A fucking moron could figure that out. Jesus. Don't they have anything to share that we don't already know?" Rachel was frustrated with the bureaucratic tripe.

"Hold on, Rachel. There's much more, and it's critical you listen carefully. CDC has been unable to establish any additional research centers. You recall they thought they were looking at Area 51. That's not going to happen. Furthermore, and this very disturbing news, *Lucifer has invaded Atlanta, our primary research center.*"

Suddenly, the atmosphere in Rachel's living room felt more like the interior of an Egyptian tomb. The trio looked at each other knowing their chances of living through the Lucifer pandemic were zip to zero.

"Atlanta is under lockdown – full-on quarantine. Lucifer somehow found its way into their level-four atmospheric filtration system. Everyone on our research team has either died or will soon expire."

David scanned the faces of his colleagues and took several deep breaths.

"Unless the Chinese or Russians have something we don't know about, we're the last bastion of mankind."

Discomposed, David shrugged his shoulders and shook his head. "I'm sad to say the rest of the world is heading for a tsunami of fatalities – nothing short of what we might expect from a cataclysmic extinction event. Except for us folks here in Keystone, the case fatality rate in PNG is virtually one hundred percent. That's about ten million men, women and children. Before Lucifer, Port Moresby had a population of about five hundred thousand people. Today, there are fewer than a few thousand, and they will shortly be included in the statistics. Lucifer continues to annihilate communities, towns, and cities on every continent. There's nowhere to hide. The fatality figures are growing exponentially."

"What about the PNG government, the police, and military?" Rachel asked.

"Gone. They no longer exist. As expected, rank has its privileges. The Prime Minister and most of his cabinet officers and upper echelon escaped to Northern Queensland or Singapore. It really didn't change the outcome. Queensland and Singapore are now on lockdown. Money can't buy you love, and it certainly can't buy your life."

David paused while parsing the abominable facts. "We're very fortunate to be here in Keystone. It's no country club, but you wouldn't want to be out there, in what is now the devil's playground. In the past, there were numerous reports of roving gangs of native men – cannibals – killing and eating anyone they captured, young or old, any gender. These men had regressed to their old customs, rituals, and myths. They sought to gain the power and wisdom of the people they ate and hoped it would appease vengeful spirits. These marauders are all dead, and there is no evidence their spirits provided refuge."

Dawson's attention was diverted by the ringtone of his phone. It was Keith Abrams, head of security. He excused himself and left the room to take the call.

"Hello, Keith. I'm in the middle of a meeting. Can I call you back?"

"Sorry to bother you, but we have a situation here at the main gate, two American missionaries, a man and a woman. They're both in their mid-twenties. They said they escaped Port Moresby three days ago on a motorcycle, spent two nights in the rainforest hiding from cannibals. They don't have any visible symptoms, but I can't let them pass without medical clearance."

"I'll alert Doctor McDermott. She'll need to test them. If they're clean, we'll find a place for them."

"And if they're infected?"

"That's up to Hemmingway. She may want to quarantine them so Quinn can test her antifungal meds on living victims."

*****

Dressed in level-four attire, Quinn and a lab tech arrived at the Keystone main entrance. The exhausted couple were seated on a nearby rock, rehydrating with bottles of fresh water and a couple of granola bars provided by the security guards.

Focusing her attention on the male, she introduced herself. "I'm Doctor McDermott. How are you feeling?"

"Exhausted, and thankful to be here. I think we'll be fine, thanks to your guards." The young man held up his nearly empty bottle of water. "We've been hiding or running from gangs of cannibals for the past two weeks. We didn't know this place existed. We just needed to get out of Port Moresby alive."

"I understand. I hope we can help. What is your name and where are you from?"

"I'm Peter Tanner. This is my girlfriend, Diane Pearson. We're both missionaries from Boise, Idaho. We hid in our church near the marina. There was food and water for a couple of weeks. But when the water ran out, we knew we had to escape. Our pastor was killed by a gang of cannibals when he went to find more water. We saw his body on the street near the church. They cut him open from his neck to his bellybutton and ate his heart and liver. There were lots of dead people, everywhere. It was horrible. Packs of wild dogs were eating them too and howling like wolves. Thank God, we had a motorcycle. That was the only way we could have escaped or made it here. The highway was jammed with trucks, cars, and dead people. We spent two nights in the rainforest. Damn mosquitos and gunfire kept us awake all night."

"You're both very lucky, and very brave. Do either of you have passports?"

"Sure, I have them in my backpack."

After confirming their identities, Quinn continued. "We need to know if either of you is infected. I need to look inside your lungs with a bronchoscope. You might feel a choking sensation, but it will not hurt and will only take a few seconds. Okay?"

Diane began to tremble while Quinn configured her test apparatus and completed her examination of Peter. With a broad smile, she proclaimed, "Peter, you're clear." Knowing she was next, Diane's heartbeat quickened, and her face turned a chalky white.

"Hey, don't worry. It's just a precaution. I don't think you're infected, but I must be certain. The lives of everyone, including you and your boyfriend, are at stake."

Diane leaned back and opened her mouth. Finding no evidence of Lucifer spores, Quinn placed her hand on Diane's shoulder. "Relax. You're clear. Welcome to Keystone."

Unleashing a gush of gratitude, Diane looked at Peter, took him by the hand and snuggled close. "We want to be together. Is that okay?"

"Absolutely," affirmed Quinn. "We have some vacant apartments. I think you'll be comfortable."

The young couple embraced. Puddles of joyful tears quickly filled their eyes and trickled down their filth-laced faces. "By the grace of God, we made it."

*****

Meanwhile, David's meeting with Dawson and Rachel continued. "Now for the bad news."

"How could it possibly get much worse than it already is?" asked Rachel.

"The USS *Kennedy* has advised they will not be able to continue to provide all the food and drinking water we've requested. It's unavailable. Their sailors have priority on their limited supplies. I don't blame them. That's how it is. They want us to become more self-sufficient. There's a growing supply of wild pigs and chickens roaming the rainforests, plus an abundance of crocodiles, which I've been told are quite tasty when cooked over an open fire. These animals, and all the others, appear to be resistant to Lucifer."

Rachel squirmed and shook her head. "No fucking way. I'm not eating the same crocs that ate humans. I'll stick to the pork and chicken and sweet potatoes."

David added his thoughts. "I'm sure we'll find a hundred ways to cook pigs and chickens. The main source of carbohydrates for the natives was sweet potatoes, and there's tons of them growing throughout the highlands. Drinking water is not a problem. We can boil river water and install rainwater catch systems if necessary. We've got plenty of rifles and ammo, helicopters, and a company of sharpshooters."

"What about gasoline, aviation fuel, propane?" Dawson queried.

"It will be rationed. We'll have to learn how to live with less. We have plenty of solar power and power storage systems to keep the lights on. We should minimize the use of propane and start using firewood for cooking. There's plenty of it in the rainforest."

"Hazmat suits don't last forever. We're going to need more of them, plus lab instrumentation, DNA tools, software, computers, chemicals," begged Rachel.

"They're all top priority. Because we're in the best possible position to discover a cure or vaccine. As much as it is available, the *Kennedy* will continue to receive medical supplies, PPE, and Lucifer research and development equipment and supplies."

David took a deep breath, pursed his lips and loudly exhaled. "Any questions?"

The room fell into a funerary silence.

CHAPTER SEVENTEEN

In their quest for a cure or vaccine, Quinn and Jonah didn't have many options. They focused their work on three areas: 1) survivability based on blood type and Rh factors, 2) developing anti-Lucifer drugs using modified variants of currently available antimalaria, antifungal, steroidal and antibiotic drugs, and 3) a longshot solution using CRISPR gene modification technology to create an organism that would consume or kill Lucifer mushrooms in situ.

Their biggest limitation was the absence of living test subjects currently infected with Lucifer. Most of their experimentation, data and analysis was based on experiments with the DNA of Lucifer mushrooms and petri dish tests using Lucifer spores and lung cells and blood from deceased victims. Their work was taxing and extremely dangerous, even with level-four PPE and stringent CDC safety protocols.

*****

Quinn had a fretful night, wracked with conflicting emotions, confusion, hope, despair, love for Tony, and heartbreak. The data didn't lie. She had repeated her test twice over. The results were undeniable. Unable to sleep and filled with angst, she rolled out of her bed and put on her sweats. Perhaps, she thought, a long workout on her stationary bike might help. After an hour and the loss of four hundred calories, she decided it was time to call Rachel and share the grim news. She quickly showered, put on a fresh pair of clothes, put on her makeup and called Rachel.

"Hi, Quinn," said Rachel, shaking the fragments of pre-dawn dreams from her brain. "It's half-past five. What's up?"

"I have the results of the blood test. We need to talk, just you and I."

"Sure. Come to my apartment. I'll put on the coffee."

Quinn gathered up her notes and rushed down the hall to Rachel's apartment.

"Hey, good morning. Sorry to wake you so early. I just... I couldn't sleep. We need to talk. It's a bit dicey."

"Hey, calm yourself. Take a deep breath. Let's get some coffee and talk in the living room."

Rachel settled into the couch next to Quinn and both women took a sip of coffee. Quinn looked uneasy. After placing her notes on the coffee table, she took a deep breath and tried to decompress.

Handing Rachel a single piece of paper she began to recite her findings. "That's a list of all the people who live in Keystone, a hundred and sixty-four."

Rachel scrutinized the list with impassioned concern.

"Jonah and I finished the first phase of our survivability study based on blood type and Rh factors. As you know, we took blood samples from everyone living inside Keystone and classified them according to blood types – A, B, AB, and O, plus the Rh positive and negative factors. Thirty-one Keystone residents are Rh negative. One hundred and thirty-three are Rh positive. The list contains the names and blood types in two columns. People with Rh positive are in the first column – Rh negative in the second column."

Rachel walked her forefinger down the list, taking mental note of those with Rh negative blood.

"Okay. So, what does this mean?" asked Rachel.

"Interestingly, the blood of our two confirmed survivors, Tony and Yvette, is type O negative. Same for the missionary couple from Idaho."

Rachel examined the list more closely. "May I keep this report?"

"Certainly, I printed it out for you to keep."

"Have you been able to draw any conclusions from this data?" Indeed, Rachel was anxious.

"Jonah and I agree that much of the online data is unverified, anecdotal, or ethnological folklore. However, there are several recent scientific reports that indicate people with type O blood are more resistant to some pathogens including malaria, candida auris, HIV, syphilis, bubonic plague, many types of influenza. Furthermore, published research papers suggest Rh negative blood is more resistant to many parasites and fungi. For example, toxoplasma gondii is a parasite that lives in the gut of house cats. Its feces contain the parasite eggs which often invade humans. Once inside the new host, it migrates to the brain, causing increasingly severe psychological problems. People with type Rh negative are immune to toxoplasma gondii. This further supports the suggestion that people with type O-negative blood may be virtually immune to Lucifer."

Frustrated, Rachel snapped. "I can read all that in your report. What I want to know is this. What is the survivability prognosis for those infected with Lucifer spores, regardless of their blood type or Rh factor?"

Susan bit her lower lip and replied. "We know the term Rh stands for rhesus factor. All apes and monkeys are Rh positive. But if all homo sapiens evolved from the same African ancestors, the great apes, why do some people have Rh negative blood? Are these people a mutation or did they evolve from some other species? Jonah and I didn't have too many options. The biggest limitation was the absence of living test subjects infected with Lucifer. Most of our survivability opinions were based on experiments with Lucifer mushroom spores and the blood samples from Keystone personnel."

Quinn took a second to reinforce her fortitude. As much as she cared not to, there was no way she could avoid telling Rachel the results. "Lucifer spores killed all the positive blood cells. I hope that answers your question."

Rachel looked up to the ceiling, then re-examined the list, struggling to believe she was as vulnerable as a hundred and thirty-two others.

"So, Lucifer did not kill the Rh negative cells?" Rachel sought a possible flaw in Quinn's data.

"Affirmative. Initially, blood type A Rh negative cells appeared distressed. But a few hours later, all the Lucifer spores had died. Blood type AB, B and O negatives showed no signs of distress whatsoever."

"Do you know why?"

"No. Jonah and I, we still need to conduct a more extensive DNA analysis, but so far, except for the Rh D antigen that is missing from Rh negative people, we have not identified any enzyme or protein in Rh negative cells that set them apart from Rh positive cells."

"Do you believe the lack of the D antigen makes a difference?"

"Our tests did not find any evidence that it did, but we need to go deeper into the DNA of people with Rh negative alleles. That will take an enormous amount of time."

"Did you try any of your anti-this, anti-that or the other experimental drugs?"

"Yes. We tried everything at our disposal. CDC may have some experimental anti-fungi, but we don't, and based on what David told us, I doubt we could get our hands on it. As for the drugs we had, the results were the same. In the presence of Lucifer spores, the only protection available to Rh positives is physical isolation, hazmat attire, and CDC protocols." Quinn reached for Rachel's hand and gently squeezed. "Hey, don't you worry. Jonah tests the outside air quality twice a day. He's never found a single Lucifer spore in the air we breathe. If you want to work in or visit the level-four lab, we've got plenty of PPE."

Quinn could tell Rachel's brain was processing the potential casualties. Her face winced, her brow frowned, wrinkles appeared at the corners of her eyes. Her lips pursed and twitched.

Rachel changed the subject. "So, what's next? What are you and Jonah planning?"

"We're going to focus on developing anti-Lucifer drugs using modified variants of currently available antimalaria, antifungal, steroidal, and antibiotic drugs. This will naturally involve extensive use of DNA analysis. And it will take time, a long time."

"And if that doesn't pan out, what's next?"

"It's a long shot, but we believe there may be a way to modify some other organisms using CRISPR gene modification technology. Our goal would be to create an organism – phages or slime mold for example – that would consume or kill Lucifer mushrooms in situ."

"Excellent. That's all we can do. You and Jonah are doing a fabulous job. If you need anything, just ask. David, Dawson, and I will do everything humanly possible to help. Let's keep this conversation between you and me, at least for a while longer."

"I'm with you," said Quinn.

Rachel cleared her throat before continuing. "If what you and Jonah have discovered is true, and I have no reason to doubt it is true, then a large percentage of humanity – perhaps as many as five billion people – those with Rh positive blood living out in the open – without protection – on every continent... *will perish*."

"I can't answer that question, Rachel."

"God, it's hard for me to wrap my head around that possibility." Rachel struggled to hold back her emotional plunge.

The two women looked eye to eye and embraced. Fresh tears welled up in their bleary eyes, filling them with sparkling liquid. Their tears cascaded down their faces –across their cheeks, and dripped off the tip of their chins.

*****

David woke up to the sing-song ring of his smartphone. It was four in the morning, a Sunday and the first day of May.

He reached for the phone and recognized the caller. It was the CDC calling from the USS *Kennedy*. He didn't know if it was good or bad news, whether to smile or growl.

"Dawson here. Who's calling?"

"David, this is Admiral Tomkins. How are you holding up?"

"Hello, Admiral. We're hanging in there as best we can. What's happening out your way?"

"I'm afraid I have some distressing news. China has recently reported hundreds of thousands of Lucifer deaths. The data is likely a week or more late. My guess over a million or more have succumbed. Goddamn bastards didn't say anything for weeks, now suddenly, they drop the nasty news. They know the epicenter is PNG. They've threatened to bomb the island with nuclear warheads."

"What the fuck are they thinking? Fucking commies. Jesus help us!"

"They believe the best way to stop the pandemic is to use nuclear weapons at the source and any other hot spots. We're trying to negotiate a softer stance, but in the absence of any reliable scientific data, or progress by your team, I don't know if we'll be able to stop them."

"How about dropping a few of our big ones on Beijing and Wuhan. Wuhan, yeah, that's where those motherfuckers created the coronavirus. They brought the entire free world to its economic knees without firing a single bullet. Yeah, we should drop a few big ones on Beijing. That should change their mindset."

"The President is on it. He's a brilliant negotiator. But the Chinese believe their entire race is doomed if Lucifer gets ahead of them."

David shuddered. He couldn't hold back the fact that there had been no progress or even a hint of a cure. He took a few moments to reply.

"They're probably right."

EPILOGUE

And it came to pass, out of eight billion humans on planet Earth, one hundred and sixty-four were living in isolation within the confines of an aging, open-pit gold mine in the central highlands of Papua New Guinea. They were surviving in a world rapidly filling with deadly mushroom spores from another place and time, spores that will ultimately kill eighty percent of the global population unless…

*****

They called it Lucifer. It had remained in a state of anhydrobiosis for billions of years, trapped in an iron sarcophagus without nutrients or water, unable to metabolize, reproduce or grow. It had survived an intergalactic collision, a journey through space and time, the explosive impact with planet Earth and three hundred million years of paralysis.

But now it was free and ready to move toward its genetic destiny. The rain infiltrated its microscopic pores and it began to rehydrate – atom by atom – cell by cell – until the entire fungal mass sprang back to life.

Dozens of threadlike mycelium tentacles slowly emerged from its body, undulating in a rhythmic motion, growing longer, searching for its first meal in billions of years. From the mycelium grew the hyphae, even smaller filaments that produced digestive exoenzymes – converting proteins into a nutritious chemical goop to be absorbed by the fungus.

As the fungus grew inside its current host, it asexually reproduced with an explosive flowering – ejecting thousands of spores into the environment. And, with the help of the wind, these microscopic spores traveled great distances before invading – and eventually killing – their next host.

ABOUT THE AUTHOR

Craig is a retired Navy SEAL, Vietnam War vet and a pioneer in the deep-sea diving industry. His underwater adventures have taken him to the deepest and most hostile parts of the world's oceans. He's worked with saturation diving systems, undersea habitats, submersibles, remote controlled underwater vehicles and experimental diving equipment. His most recent books take the reader on a magical journey into the world of predictive science-fiction. Grounded in empirical scientific and technological advances, his speculative fiction thrillers provide insight into the terrifying dynamics of Mother Nature and the apocalyptic pestilence mankind may encounter during the next twenty years. Craig lives in Southern California with his wife, Lynn.

WEB SITE: www.craigmarley.com

NO LIFEGUARD ON DUTY

Legacy of a Navy SEAL

CRAIG MARLEY

TALKING DOLPHINS Series

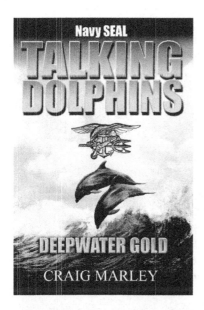

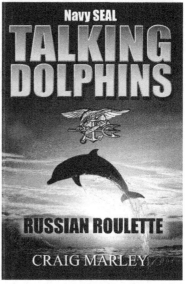

SPECULATIVE FICTION

Made in the USA
Coppell, TX
13 June 2021

57381729R00115